R O

Rose Boyt was born in 1958. Her first novel, *Sexual
Intercourse*, was published in 1989. She is currently
working on her third novel.

Rose Boyt

ROSE

VINTAGE

VINTAGE
20 Vauxhall Bridge Road, London SW1V 2SA

London Melbourne Sydney Auckland Johannesburg
and agencies throughout the world

First published by Chatto & Windus Ltd, 1991
Vintage edition 1992

1 3 5 7 9 10 8 6 4 2

Printed and bound in Great Britain by
Cox & Wyman Ltd, Reading

ISBN 0 09 988930 7

DREAMBOAT

I have developed a taste for big men that in practice has never been satisfied. It's not that there is a shortage of big men. There are plenty of them around. It's just that at the point when assignations are made, when my eye is level with a nipple poking blindly through the stretched fabric of a white tee-shirt, when I am held in arms long enough to encircle me twice, when I crane my neck to get a glimpse of the face I assume is smiling (and beyond it I can see the spinning mirrored ball spattering the dancefloor with gobs of light, or later on, if he takes me outside, the melancholy paleness of the moon at dawn), in short when his erect penis is thrust against my stomach, I take fright and slip away.

It was painful to see the man hurt my mother. The man was a German. His name was Klaus. He had a whim one day at sea to order from the galley a dish of sausage and cabbages to remind him of his homeland. I sat with my mother in the galley as she quartered cabbages and cut out their white hearts. The dish

3

was unfamiliar to us. She shared her uncertainty with me; the red hand holding the knife was unsteady and she asked me, 'Shall I slice it? Should it be sliced?'

'Don't slice it,' I said. I did not like to see her wield the knife. Together we piled the sausages and cabbages into the saucepan. My mother heaved it onto the stove.

The galley began to sweat with the smell of those cabbages. It was a terrible smell. I climbed up on a stool and peered into the huge saucepan. The sausages lay diminished and flaccid on a bed of greasy leaves.

When dinner was served, the man peered into the saucepan as I had done, and his lip, stretched in a disgusted grimace, was pearled with drops of condensation. The crew laughed. Wordlessly he lifted the saucepan off the table and poured its contents overboard into the sea. Gulls dropped screaming out of the sky to feed.

That night as I lay in my bunk weeping for the sorrow of my mother she came to me and kissed away my tears.

'He was seasick,' she said. 'He threw away the food because he was too sick to eat. He was seasick and ashamed.'

I knew that she could not bear to see me cry for her. Better to mock the man. Better to laugh at him and take away his sealegs. We laughed together in the candlelight. And what if it were true? Was the man sick and ashamed? A storm pitched the ship in blackness. He was the captain. We were in his hands.

I have developed a horror of big men. I am not saying that they throw themselves at me. They can take me or leave me. It's just that if, one solitary night, the giant in my head was made flesh by the scent of my longing and pounced I would die.

How unbearable to meet him again, to meet him in some layby on the A202, my neck stiff from driving, his neck coarse and shaven, caught in my headlamps, on the way to the sea. Should I feel pity? I could run him over. I would take fright and drive away.

I knew it would be Christmas when we arrived in Denmark. I felt no sadness as we left England behind us; it was a thin line and then the little lights faded away. I leant over the stern of the ferry to watch the boiling of the water and then turned, my face wet, to climb over coils of oily rope and listen to my footsteps slapping on the deck. My mother held the youngest child in her arms. He was a baby of nine or ten months, a boy called Conrad, golden-haired like Klaus, blue-eyed, folded in a knitted shawl. My mother called out to me.

'Hold onto Flora's hand, darling.'

So I had to hold hands with my sister. Her little hand was warm and soft in mine. The other child, the oldest, was a boy. His name was Louis. He sat down in a coil of rope.

'We are going to Christmas,' he said.

When we arrived the snow was deep and we rode on a sleigh. I heard the sleigh-bells ringing. My mother walked beside us, carrying the baby, leaving tidy footprints in the snow. The baby's face was hidden. You could not see the shape of its tiny limbs or the outline of its back or head inside the shawl, and yet because of the tender way she cradled the bundle in her arms you could tell what it contained. I was looking for reindeer. An old man pulled the sleigh, his back bent under the rope across his shoulder. I wanted to walk, to get my weight off his back, but as we slipped along in the frozen grey quietness I was unable to speak.

The path was broad and smooth between the banks of snow that gleamed in the light of the old man's lantern. I looked for reindeer and Father Christmas and Jesus and God in the shadows because it was Christmas. Beneath the branches of pines in the distance I searched for eyes. I dared them to wink at me. My stare was belligerent. My mother was smiling. Her face was pale and smiling into the darkness. The moon rose and rimed her hair with silver.

So we slid through the moonlight into the forest. I held my breath. The forest was breathing. Boughs reached out of the darkness to touch my cheek or catch my hair in trailing fingers. I held my mittened hand across my eyes. The lantern-light blackened the shadows. Our silence served to amplify the sighing of the trees.

My sister crouched beside me in the sledge, wrapped in a tartan travelling rug, her teeth chattering. I peeped out at her. Goosepimples puckered the exposed skin of her cheek, and her chin, a dimpled mound of rosy flesh, trembled with the effort she was making to keep her mouth closed. I was untouched; her brave little face irritated me. I savoured the irritation because it saved me from the strange beauty of the forest. I stuck my tongue out at my sister and kept my head down.

And then I heard my mother singing.

'Good King Wenceslas looked out, on the feast of Stephen.
When the snow lay round about, deep and crisp and even.'

My brother and sister joined in. I raised my eyes and saw that the sleigh was carrying us into a golden bower where my mother was dancing. Her hair was haloed with gold. My fear no longer peopled the shadows with lurking things. My mother carried the lantern and led us singing out of the forest.

Then I saw the ship, the great hull black against the dark water, her masts bone-white against the sallow sky.

The man kissed my mother and kissed the baby. I heard my mother make a soft cooing noise like a dove. The baby began to cry.

I remember the man's smell. He knelt to face me. I lowered my eyes.

'Look at me,' he said.

I looked at him. His blue eyes were brimming with sentiment.

'Sweet Rose,' he said.

I felt sick. He was smiling at me. He was trying to melt me with his smile.

'Hello,' I said, and he laughed.

I knew he was going to kiss me. I shut my eyes. He kissed me on the lips.

The mate appeared out of the fo'c'sle, a gauntleted ogre, snorting, black-bearded, shouting at the captain. I assumed that the guttural noises issuing out of his mouth were some nautical language as yet unknown to me, a language I longed to understand, of ships and the sea. I moved my lips in imitation of him but produced only a caustic barking that he took as mockery and silenced with a glare. My mother caught me flinching. She touched the back of my neck with her cold fingers to comfort me and spoke.

'He is speaking Danish,' she said.

'What is he saying?' I asked.

'I don't know,' said Mother.

The captain spoke to the mate in English.

'Pay the old bastard,' he shouted.

I turned and saw behind me the sleigh man holding out his hand.

'Yes, sir,' said the mate, descending the gangplank and pulling off a glove. He searched in his pockets for money. His pockets were full of miscellaneous objects that he removed one by one and placed in a pile on the outstretched palms of my brother, who was standing by his side. My brother's face was grave. I grew nervous. The mate's deliberation was a taunt to the captain in which my brother was implicated. My brother's face was blissful. He held in his hands a marlin spike, a ball of oiled twine, a belaying pin, a cigarette lighter, a knife. The captain shouted at the mate. My mother opened the clasp of her bag and drew out of its calf-lined interior a handful of coins. She gave them to the sleigh man. He bowed to her and went on his way.

The mate grinned as he stuffed his belongings back into his pockets. I thought he might leave one of the smaller objects in the hands of my brother as payment, a mark of his esteem, a gift – but he did not. My brother's hands were empty. I looked for traces of disappointment in his face but there were none. Perhaps it was enough for him to have touched the contents of the mate's pockets and to have been of service.

I saw him raise his cold blue palms to his nose and sniff. He was breathing in the smell of oiled twine, the smell of greased metal, the mate's smell, the ship.

Then we climbed the gangplank, a narrow bridge over the water, and heard beneath us in the darkness the licking of the sea. The sodden fenders creaked in the fissure like bodies pressed between the ship and shore. I reached for my mother's hand. The hand that caught mine was unfamiliar; I looked up and made out above me in the light of the ship's lantern the face of Veronica. She winked at me.

The ship was made of wood, sea-bleached and salted, the deck worn smooth by scrubbing and the tread of many feet. I stood at the base of a mast growing out of the deck like a tree and tried to encircle it with my arms; I stretched myself but my fingers would not meet; nor would the arms of the man have closed round that massive trunk. My cheek was laid against it.

The smell made me close my eyes. I held the mast in my embrace, my lips parting, and the mast held me until my mother came and drew me away.

She led me and I followed. The ship was empty now; I could see no one and yet I could hear voices, the voices of my brother and sister, echoing up from under my feet as if from under the sea.

'Come on,' said my mother. 'Mind your head. Come on. Follow me.'

She ducked under the swathed boom and began to disappear into a hole in the deck. I went after her and saw below me a steep staircase leading down from the hatch into the gloom of the hold, and Mother's face, smiling up at me out of the darkness. She was descending backwards, receding, leaving me behind on the deck with the boom, furled in pale sailcloth, creaking above my head.

'Come on, dear,' she said.

The descent into the hold was a slow one; I was seven years old, a timid child, and to lower myself blindly into the hole, to dangle my toes into the cavernous darkness, toes I would never allow to stick out from under the blankets, even at home, in my own little bed, for fear of losing them to some beast who might have been hiding in the dusty gap between the bedstead and the floor, was not easy for me. I was about halfway down when I felt myself caught under the armpits and swung to the ground.

'There we are,' said my mother. 'There's a good girl. Look!'

I opened my eyes. It was a forest. The air was unctuous, dank, fragrant with the sap of fir trees, hundreds of them, dense and abundant, growing under the sea. Red ribbons looped and trailed through their branches, threaded with haloed hearts and lustrous stars of plaited straw. Veronica wandered in the forest, crowned with tinsel and silver paper, waving a lighted taper like a wand. Tongues of fire spat in the damp, poking out of the green-black branches – there was a smell of candlegrease – and then the flames blossomed, you could see that the candles were yellow, the flames bloomed like golden flowers in the forest, and Veronica, her tinsel crown gleaming, vanished.

In a clearing in the forest, carpeted with pale tarpaulin, on a table, long, narrow and low, there was an enormous cake, taller than I was, spun out of eggwhite and sugar, a column of confectionery, layer upon layer, melting slightly in the damp of the ship's hold, in the green gloom of the forest, the centrepiece of a magnificent feast. I sat on a little stool at the table and saw before me, written in silvery ink, a card bearing my name. My name was written in icing on a gingerbread heart. My initial was embroidered on the corner of a napkin. I picked up my plate and read the words painted round the rim. Happy Christmas Rose.

My brother and sister joined me at the table, their faces smudged and wan after the long journey, and we looked with big eyes at the food; it was a feast so tempting and lavish – armies of chocolate Father Christmases, heaps of pastries, sugared almonds, bananas, tangerines – and put together with so little regard for proper nourishment, that we were afraid to touch it. We pulled crackers; I crowned my sister with a hat of coloured paper, and my brother wore a plastic moustache attached to the inside of his nose with little pincers. It made him look like Hitler. The paper hat slipped down over my sister's eyes and we laughed. I heard my mother laughing in the forest. I was tired and hungry and I thought I was in fairyland. Then the man appeared, wearing a big white beard made out of cotton wool and a dress made out of a red curtain.

'Father Christmas,' said my little sister.

'Ho ho ho,' said the man. 'Eat up little children.'

My mother gave me a paintbox for Christmas, a metal one with an enamelled palette that folded out to reveal a double row of cubed and labelled colours, their top surfaces convex like satin cushions, fitted into neat white frames – indigo, cobalt, ultramarine, viridian, forest, chrome, ochre, umber, cerise, carmen, scarlet, white. I scratched my name on the bottom of the paintbox with a pin.

I painted the fairies whom I believed inhabited the wood-yard I had found at the back of the harbour on the way to the post office, fairies full-skirted and gossamer-winged, similar in appearance to the angel on top of the school Christmas tree we had left behind us in London, and yet more corporeal, more cherubic and rosy-cheeked like our baby.

The fairies were bathed in moonlight. The night sky was a density of indigo, the unstable pigment bleeding into green, and I discovered a way to paint the moon. It was unsatisfactory painting a white disk over the blue – the white paint was chalky, flat, and lacked luminosity; I tried yellow, yellow running into blue – a cheesy moon, a green moon, a moon that spread, as I tried to make the outline perfect, and hung, blurred and ugly, six feet above the ground, or shrunk into insignificance. The answer was to leave a gap in the indigo, an absence of paint, a moon of nothingness more real than its painted counterparts. I discovered that an unpainted moon would shine. It would keep its distance in the back of the sky, remote and strange, a gap holding in its lack of substance an intimation of real moonishness.

The man gave me a book for Christmas, a square book, its pages blank and daunting, inviting, in which to write my thoughts. The cover was made of stiff plastic, violent roses blooming on a white background, in the style of shower curtains, yellow and red. You could lock up the book like a box; a little heart-shaped padlock dangled open from the clasp; and in the keyhole was a tiny key.

I called the book my diary. I sat down on January the first at the long table in the main cabin and wrote *MY DIARY* on the first page. My brother was sitting next to me. He had a book like mine, except that the cover was different. The cover of his book was decorated with an abstract design in blue and brown and his padlock was not heart-shaped. He opened his book and wrote *MY JOURNAL* on the first page. I could not think of anything to write so I watched him. He was writing in joined-up. The long looped strokes of the tall letters leaned forward as if about to fall over.

'Come on Rose,' said my mother. 'Make an effort.'

My mother was sitting in a big chair at the end of the table.

'I can't think of anything,' I said.

'What have you done today?'

'Nothing,' I said.

My brother's hand crept across his page. I watched him make the words slowly. *ROSE IS A FAT PIG. SHE IS UGLY AND GREEDY. I HATE HER.*

'Mum,' I said. 'It's not fair. Look. Look what he is writing.'

'Get on with your own work,' said Mother.

So I sharpened my pencil and wrote: *January the first. I hate my brother. Today we had herring for breakfast. I hate herring.* I leaned back and chewed the end of my pencil, overcome by the ineffable boredom of writing.

'Please read out your work,' said my mother.

'Rose is a fat pig,' said Louis.

'I hate my brother,' I said.

'Darlings!' my mother cried.

I turned and spat in my brother's face. He punched me on the upper arm.

'Stop it,' said my mother.

'She pinched me,' said my brother.

'He punched me,' I said.

'Stop it!' my mother screamed.

We stopped.

'Now,' said my mother, drawing a nappy pin out of the front of her jersey. She held the sharp point of the pin in the flame of a match.

'Hold out your hands.'

We did as we were told. She took my brother's thumb in her hand and drew blood. She took my thumb in her hand and drew blood. She made us press our two thumbs together so that the blood mixed.

'That's better,' she said.

We licked our small wounds clean.

'Blood brother. Blood sister,' she said. 'Now get back to your work.'

I watched my brother write. *Today the Selma went on the slips. The bosun gave me an old coin.*

I could not think of anything to write. The page was so small and bare. I tried to draw a picture of a seagull but it went wrong. It looked more like a little dog or a seal. I don't know what happened to that diary. I wrote in it every day until it was full. I lost the heart-shaped padlock and I lost the little key. My mother still has my brother's journal, and sometimes, for instance at Christmas, when the family is gathered together, she brings it down from the flat box on top of the wardrobe and everyone laughs at the childish entries. *ROSE IS A FAT PIG. SHE IS UGLY AND GREEDY. I HATE HER.*

That is how I remember it. I was fat and ugly. My sister has a photograph of me at the age of seven or eight sunning my legs on the deck of our ship. At first when she showed me the photograph I did not recognise my legs. I recognised my saucy little face and the faded pinafore I used to wear, but the legs I could not remember at all. I thought that they must belong to Veronica. The legs are elegant and womanly. What happened to that little girl? I wonder at the discrepancy between my memory of myself as a child and the image of myself as a child in the photograph. Veronica's face in the photograph means nothing to me. The events of the story have rubbed it out. And yet in spite of this erasure I retain on my heart a shadow of her love.

So we became blood brother and blood sister, my brother and I. What impressed me most about the ritual was not the exchange of blood; after all I already shared the same blood as my brother and this did not stop him from tormenting me; no, I was impressed by my mother's readiness to pierce the tender ball of my thumb, her ruthless keenness to wound me. The solemnity of the ritual transformed my mother into a savage. She lost her soft and yielding smile. The ritual smelt to me of punishment and I read in the dilation of her eyeball a glint of pleasure. Still I noticed, now that I was joined to my brother by this brutal and romantic bond, that he hated me less, perhaps because we had been wounded together.

She went fishing for eels in the middle of the night. At dusk the mate lowered the lifeboat that hung on a rope-and-pulley system at the stern of our ship and moored it alongside. We were already in our bunks when Mother climbed down the rope ladder and took her place in the bows of the little boat, spear at the ready, the sail set, her torch flashing across the water. The man, Klaus, manned the tiller.

They returned at dawn. Mother was almost unrecognisable, clothed in oilskins, her hair tied back with a length of string, her face moony like the face of a murderer, a pronged spear in her hand.

'Did you catch anything?' I asked, awake suddenly now she had returned. My mother held up an eel in a net bag.

'Yes,' she said.

The eel was still alive.

'Let's eat it for breakfast,' said my mother.

To me it looked unappetising. I dressed quickly and followed her into the galley. She emptied the eel out of its string bag onto the table and together we watched it writhing.

'You'd better kill it,' I said.

Mother sharpened a knife.

'Cut off its head,' I said.

She tried to grasp the eel in her hand. Its mottled skin was coated in a slimy lubrication – it left a bluish smear on Mother's fingers when she withdrew them.

'I can't,' she said. 'I can't.'

'Give me the knife,' I said.

I held the eel down with a dry cloth wrapped around my hand and sawed off its head. It continued to writhe.

'It's still alive,' I said.

Out of the severed head a cluster of entrails was hanging, slate-blue, bile-green, and liverish.

'I know!' said Mother. 'Let's cook it whole.'

She put a black frying pan onto the stove and lit the gas.

'It's all right,' I said. 'I can cut it.'

I hacked the eel into four pieces, caught the pieces up in the cloth and shook them out into the pan.

'Look,' I said.

The pieces were still wriggling as they fried. Then at last they were still. It was a delicious smell that rose out of the frying pan. Then we ate.

It was not just the fish in the sea that were alive; the fishmonger in Marstal sold cod out of an aquarium. In the dense salt water their bodies touched – pale underbelly and iridescent cheek, bristling fin and blackened spine – and the surface of the water was broken. They swam slowly, confined in their tank. Their eyes were gormless.

'Which one shall we have?' asked Mother.

It was difficult to choose. They were all of a similar size and wore on their fishy lips similar expressions of cunning that belied the seeming oblivion in their eyes. Clearly it was not a question of the beauty of their markings as when buying goldfish. My sister liked the one that lurked at the bottom of the tank and nosed the glass.

'Look, it's sweet,' she said, pointing.

'It's not for a pet,' I said.

'It's for dinner,' said my brother.

'Stupid,' I added.

'Fish face.'

'Ssh,' said my mother. 'Look.'

A fish leapt out of the water, as if trying to escape, splashing water onto the fish-shop floor.

'That one,' I said.

'Yes.'

'Yes.'

'It's a brute,' said my mother.

The fishmonger caught it in a net. It was a good three feet long. My mother carried it home thrashing in her shopping bag. That afternoon, as I was dressing my Sindy doll in a sleeveless floral mini-dress my mother had made for her out of a scrap of engine rag, I heard a yelp of fear from the galley. I dropped my doll onto the floor of the cabin and ran.

When I reached the galley steps I saw through the open door the cod flapping about on the woven plastic mat between the table and the stove. My mother, knife in hand, was backing away from the cod towards the sink as though it would bite her.

'I thought it was dead,' she said. 'It was lying on the table. It wasn't moving. I was just about to cut it open. It gave me a fright,' she said.

The fish was dying. Its tail slapped feebly on the mat. It lay still. I prodded it with the toe of my boot.

'That's it. It's dead,' I said.

'Thank God,' said Mother.

She lifted the fish onto the table and slit it from its wastehole to its gills. Milky roe spilt out of the gash. My mother cut off its head. And then, in imitation of suicide, with a flourish and a grimace, she drew the bloodied knife across her own white throat. She made a salivary creaking noise out of the side of her mouth.

'Stop it!' I shouted. I saw myself orphaned.

She laughed. 'Sorry, only a joke.'

As she salted and peppered the gaping gutted fish I bit my lip until it bled to hold back my tears.

At seven o'clock it was time for my baby brother to go to bed. My mother bathed him in an enamel basin and laid him on a folded towel and sprinkled him with powder. She showed me how to fold the nappy and shield the baby from the pin. He wore a white flannel vest fastened to one side with ribbon ties and a stripy woollen sleeping suit, red and white. My mother carried him over her shoulder into his cabin, gave him his feed and kissed him goodnight. She was in the habit of sitting with him until he fell asleep because if she left the room while he was still awake he began to cry. I waited for her in the main cabin. Then I heard her calling me.

'Rose,' she whispered.

I tiptoed to his cabin door.

'Sit with the baby for me tonight.'

I took her place on the stool beside my brother's bunk and sang to him and stroked his back. He did not seem to notice the change. I wanted to pick him up and squeeze him in my arms but I knew that he would wake up. So I sat with him and watched his eyes close and open and close.

I have no children.

Last night as I sat alone in my room, my feet up on the seat of a chair, a cup of tea by my elbow, a cigarette held away from me so that the smoke would not get up my nose, daydreaming, as I am accustomed to do, the telephone rang. It was my mother, telling me that I have become an auntie. Auntie Rose. I could not think who had given birth.

'It's a boy,' said my mother.

I hoped that my ignorance would not be taken as a sign of deficient interest in family life on my part, or worse still a manifestation of old-maidish envy, dressed up as indifference, a trait I may be developing, although I am only twenty-eight, and which I am keen either to disguise or to make into a joke. Anyway the child turned out to be the offspring of my half-brother's half-sister. They called the baby Klaus. My half-brother's half-sister sent a photograph of the baby to my mother. She told me last night that it was displayed on her mantelpiece in a little frame.

When I am driving along in my Ford Cortina, the window wound down, my glasses (horn-rimmed) perched on the bridge of my nose (I am steering casually with one hand, the car is an automatic), I can see everything – my neighbour's husband outside the off-licence groping up the skirt of her best friend, the rolled-up trouser-leg of the man who jumped off the block of flats opposite Trellick Towers and lived, a woman carrying a flat box of chicken wings out of Ahmed Butchers, an architect in a Citroën Safari, a man I hate, his eyes hidden under the peak of his cap, stooping so that his face is almost level with mine and mouthing at me through the window of my car.

'Give me your pussy. I want to fuck you and suck you. Let me stick my finger up you.'

I turn on the radio. Walk This Way. If You Let Me Stay. A man in a wheelchair circles in a stream of urine issuing out of his shoe.

I double-park at the end of Cambridge Gardens to pick up my washing. I knew that woman when she was young. She has three kids, no teeth, a tan.

'All right, babes? You courting? Nice. You'll be next.'

The hand with which she pats her stomach is ringed and brown. I said goodbye and walked back to my car, cradling the bag of washing in my arms.

'Why don't you have another baby?'

'I am, darling. Look at me!'

'Whose baby is that, Mummy, the one in the cradle by the side of your bed?'

'It's mine of course, darling. Ours.'

'Oh no. Not another baby, Mum.'

'Don't say that, darling. Look at her. She's so sweet.'

'The baby's crying.'

'Poor little thing. Please help me.'

'They're your bloody kids, Mum. You look after them.'

'Don't be cruel, darling. I only have to look at a naked man to get pregnant. I didn't know the facts of life until it was too late. I tried to get an abortion but they wouldn't give me one. Anyway the only time I really feel myself is when I've got one on the way.'

'Don't, Mum. Please stop crying.'

'I can't help it. You are so cruel and heartless.'

'Stop crying or I will call an ambulance.'

It's safe inside my car, my four-door saloon, cocoon, my padded cell (upholstered in blue brushed nylon, the doors shag-piled) – my room. And if I am immobilised, one sultry afternoon, in a tailback on the Westway, say, or in the crawling chaos of a pile-up, bumper to bumper, sweating in a carbon monoxide haze, I can always bale out, make a run for it, abandoning my car in the middle of the road with its door open and the engine running, while I haul myself over the barrier, showing my knickers to the passers-by, the barrier that separates the motionless traffic from the stream of pedestrians in which I lose myself.

It's safe inside my car. The man in the car in front of me is adjusting his rear-view mirror. I can see nothing in the mirror but his eyes.

My father's car was as long as a hearse. It used to make me sick riding in the back of it. I would watch my colour changing out of the corner of my eye in the small slanted mirrors that lured me, as they gleamed in their padded alcoves beside the back windows, with the splendour of their very existence; embedded in frames of plushy felt they winked at me like eyes. I saw myself fading and knew, by the time I was taking my seat opposite my father at the table of the restaurant, that my face was green.

He held me in his arms at a tall window that overlooked a square and trees. He was singing to me. You great big beautiful doll. Let me put my arms around you, I'm so glad I found you. My mother was washing a lettuce under a running tap. My brother and sister were sitting at the table, my sister in a high-chair, waiting for lunch. You great big beautiful doll. That was me. My father was holding me in his arms. I was sitting on his forearm, my legs dangling, looking out of the window. Then he put me down and slipped away.

After that first Christmas in Denmark the harbour at Marstal froze. The ice, an expanse of whiteness, lay across the water a foot thick, and the ship was immobilised. It floated in a hole in the ice kept open by the ship's small movements. The hole was big enough to take a bucket dropped over the side on the end of a rope. The captain was keen to harden us up, to make us brave and unashamed in preparation for the thaw and our ensuing journey. We appeared naked on deck each morning, shaking and screaming, so he could douse us one by one with water freshly drawn out of the sea. He told us that it was good to be clean and strong and free. The sea would impart to us its power. Down below in the main cabin my mother or Veronica would chafe our blue bodies after the bath and wrap us in towels and give us cups of hot sweet tea. I tried to feel clean and strong and free. I wanted to please Klaus. I wanted to be brave so that he would love me. Klaus drank Tabasco sauce neat out of the bottle and ate raw eggs, shell and all. I wanted the power of the sea.

He taught me the warning signal for the arrival of the customs men (three short buzzes on the buzzer wired up outside my cabin door) and made it my duty to see that the main cabin was ready for inspection by the time the inspectors descended from the deck to look around. Klaus said he would be able to keep them talking on deck for two minutes at the most and so that was the time-limit for the operation. As soon as the buzzer went off I grabbed the dustpan and brush hanging from a nail inside the door of the linen cupboard and set to work, brushing down the table and benches of the main cabin, sweeping the floor, emptying ashtrays, throwing empty bottles into the bin. Klaus showed me how to scatter toys across the table and arrange open storybooks among them to give an impression of family life. I learnt how to slide shut the false back of the linen cupboard, hiding the secret place where Klaus stowed away his supply of spirits and cigarettes. I learnt how to stack up piles of sheets and towels in the front part of the linen cupboard, hiding the sliding door. Klaus would press the buzzer without warning at any time of the day or night, to keep me on my toes. Then he would stand over me with his stopwatch as I got under the table with the dustpan and brush. At first his anger at my ineptitude upset me, but once I was able to complete Operation Contraband, as he called it, in less than two minutes he rewarded me with one of his smiles. The sense of complicity made me swoony and breathless – I was glad that he had singled me out.

Across the ice in the distance a flight of swans alighted in the shelter of the harbour wall. Only their bills and feet were clearly visible, drawn against the snow – their plumage was white as the ice. I used to watch them from the roof of the deckhouse, perched on the frozen casing of a winch. I had assumed that swans were flat-bottomed, seeing them glide on the Serpentine. I had not thought that they had feet. Those grounded swans made me dream.

It was hard to get to sleep lying in my narrow bunk below the surface of the sea, the sighs of ice shifting somewhere above my head and the snores of my sister sleeping in the bunk below mine marking out the perimeter of my own silence; I was buried in a sheath of blankets but was unable by this method to obliterate my sense of the world beyond me; the more I sought to swoon out of it into my own quietness the more clamorous it became

– I heard the ship's timbers grinding against the nails that pierced them and the groan of rivets straining in her ribs; I heard the whistling of the mate on deck and the soft voices of my mother and Klaus purring in the main cabin where they slept together in the big wooden bed. Their voices ran together harmoniously, descant and bass, out of their two mouths into one chord that insinuated itself out of their bed into mine, into my ears that were cocked to receive it. I pressed the palms of my hands over my ears. I counted each intake of breath, each exhalation, my fingers, my toes. And yet each time I felt myself slipping away from the ship and the sea I leapt in my bunk in recoil from the drop into sleep, from that fall, through the quietness I desired, into the drowning sea of dreams that awaited me, colder far and deeper than the harbour sea at Marstal lying quietly beneath its slab of ice. I woke up trembling, I counted my fingers and toes, and finally I slept.

I dreamt I was walking across the frozen sea towards the harbour wall, and the swans. Snow powdered the ice, a drifted sprinkling soft like down and warm, cossetting my dipping feet and rising in clouds about my ankles. A wisp floated upwards, passed through my parted lips and settled on my tongue, where it lay like spun sugar and melted. I tried to swallow the juice but there was too much of it; some of it dribbled down my chin. From the harbour wall I could hear mewing, and the small sound pierced me – a lost creature was crying out, it was calling me. Beyond the snowdrift that contained in its hollows the sleeping swans, their necks curved and graceful, their eyelashes sweeping their cheeks, I saw a baby swan, a bundle of gorgeous soft feathers, sobbing in the snow. I picked up the downy bird and placed it inside my coat. As I carried it back to the ship I began to feel its weight and the warmth it transferred to me, nestling close to my heart. The swan was mine. I took it with me into my bunk and slept with it folded in my arms. I would protect it. It would love me. But when I woke up it was gone. I woke up in the black of night and saw that I had been dreaming. My loss made me cry out. Then I bore my loss blankly in silence until dawn. Tears came with the first light and my resolve to go out on the ice. I would find a baby swan and keep it for a pet. I would love it. It would love me. I cried myself to sleep.

It was nine o'clock when my mother woke me.

'Lazybones,' she said, kissing me on the forehead.

'I want to go on the ice,' I said. 'Take me on the ice.'

'Ask Veronica,' said Mother. 'I'm too busy.'

I dressed myself and found Veronica in the deckhouse, staring out of the window across the harbour to the sea.

'Take me on the ice,' I said.

'Please,' said Veronica.

'Please. I want to feed the swans. The poor swans,' I said.

Mother gave me a bag of stale crusts and wrapped my head up in a scarf.

'Off you go. Be careful. Be good,' she said.

Veronica took my hand and led me down the slippery gangplank onto the snowy shore. The snow was so thick you could hardly make out the steps dropping down from the harbour into the sea.

'Careful,' said Veronica.

I followed her, treading the smooth flat places where she had trodden. She had to place her feet on the steps at an angle so that the toes of her boots would not overhang. The ice spread vast and white before us. We stood together on the last step; the rest of the steps were frozen under the sea.

'One, two, three, go!' I said.

That was it. We were walking across the ice towards the harbour wall.

It was not very different from walking on dry land. I had expected to be afraid, to see through the ice as through glass to the fish and the sea, to slip on its brilliance, to hear it crack beneath my weight, but a night fall of snow lay on the surface, crisp and blinding, a crust in which we safely sank our feet.

I made a snowball in my gloved hand and lamely tossed it at Veronica. It broke up on her back. She turned and smiled at me, waiting for me to catch up, holding out her hand. I took it and we walked in silence. Then she spoke.

'The swans,' she said.

I looked up and saw them. They were coarse and unclean.

'Walk slowly,' said Veronica. 'Don't frighten them.'

I chucked a crust of bread into their midst but they disdained it.

'They are afraid,' said Veronica, as we advanced.

Then they began to hiss. They stuck out their necks and opened their beaks and hissed at me. I emptied the rest of the bread out of the bag. It made a terrible mess of crumbs in the snow. The swans were brutish and ungrateful. There were no cygnets.

'Let's go,' I said.

Later on that day when I was lying on my bed sulking because of my disappointment I overheard Veronica talking to my mother. I knew that she was talking about me. She was telling my mother that my poor little heart was broken. Veronica understood me. She had long golden hair. I loved her.

When I bit my sister Klaus tried to spank me. I ran away because the fight was between my sister and myself – I did not want him to join in – and besides she had started it. I scrambled into my bunk and waited for him. I knew that he would come and get me. Panting, I hid under the covers. I held onto them but he ripped them out of my grasp. I cringed in my nightgown, his hot breath on my face. I screamed. He caught hold of my ankles (I was lying on my back) and forced them back over my head. My naked bottom was level with his face. The little labia opened to reveal reddened membranes. I could feel his moist breath warming me. His hand was poised to spank me. And then I heard the calming voice of my mother.

'Klaus,' she said.

He let go of my ankles and my legs snapped back onto the bunk.

'Mummy,' I wailed. 'Mummy.'

I held out my arms and my mother flew into them. I peeped out from behind her shoulder and saw Klaus shamefacedly taking his leave and I smiled.

After supper Mother left us in the galley, the table loaded with unwashed plates, the sink full of dirty saucepans, the crew passing round a cloth to wipe the grease from their mouths and hands, Veronica sitting on Kurt's knee drinking a bottle of Coca-Cola through a straw, Klaus and the bosun discussing the causes of flatulence, Flora eating a slice of bread and jam, Louis whittling a piece of wood with Klaus's knife, me holding the baby on my knee. Klaus looked at Mother as she left, her shoulders rigid, hunched in anger, and shrugged. We heard her descend the stairs and potter about below. After a few minutes I followed her, the baby supported on one hip. I looked in the main cabin but Mother was not there. I found her in the cabin I shared with Flora, curled up on her side in my little bunk. As I entered she raised her hands to cover her face but I saw her red nose and gaping mouth. She was crying, swallowing deep wet sobs of breath, her knees pressed up against her breasts. The sucked breaths welling up in her chest made her shake. I waited for the noisy exhalation. It sounded almost as if Mother were coughing when she let go. The stifled cries that escaped were rhythmic, insistent, squealing. Once her chest was empty there was a hollow instant of muteness, too long, before the next sob. I tried to comfort her by stroking her head gently with my free hand but she shook her head and continued to cry. I wondered whether my attentions were unwelcome, I wondered whether I should leave her. I tried not to cry. I thought that she would prefer me to stay with her even if my caresses were unacknowledged. I did not want to leave her. I thought it would be better for her not to be alone.

The baby was a dear sweet-smelling thing, pink and dimpled, small and clean, but we were filthy – filthy black-necked children, the hair birdnested on our heads, the dirt ingrained. The daily saline dousing was endured in vain.

'Look at you!' Klaus shouted.

We bowed our heads.

'You are disgusting! You are unclean!'

It was true. He tried to scrub us down on deck with soap and a rag but we would not submit to the agony of the abrasive cloth. We escaped him, slithering out of his lathered hands, leaping mad with cold. He was forced to admit that the deck-baths were ineffective. He was used to giving orders.

'Take these filthy children to the bath-house,' he shouted.

So every Monday morning we set off across the little frozen port. My mother carried the baby, and beside her walked Veronica, holding hands with my sister, carrying in her free hand a large straw bag of clean clothes. My brother and I meandered out in front, taking turns on our shared bicycle where the snow was packed enough to ride on, taking turns to push it where the snow was too soft. We left Mother and Veronica far behind, but we could hear them calling to us.

'Rose!'

'Louis!'

'Don't go too fast, darlings!'

My mother's call was musical, rising, swooping like a little song. Veronica was husky like a film star. I imitated my mother in reply.

'Loueeee. Daaarlings.'

I made my brother laugh. He threw a snowball at me. I fell off the bike. We lay together laughing in the snow, giving the others a chance to catch up.

'Get up, you'll get cold,' said Mother.

My brother jumped onto the bicycle and I chased after him as he cycled away.

The hilarity we shared as we snowballed and skidded through Marstal died on us suddenly as we took our places at the back of a shivering queue. It was mostly old women, I thought that they must have been witches or widows, old women whose heads were swathed in woollen wrappings, queueing patiently, bowed and silent, as if in deference to the stony grandeur of the bath-house or the ritual of the bath. It was impossible to imagine that those nodding old birds would emerge from their dingy coverings and plunge naked into the water, those women whose silence silenced us, who were too reserved even to speak. They must have known each other, those grandmothers of that little town. They must have shared secrets in the queue at the post office, they must have exchanged greetings and cards at Christmas. But now in view of their imminent nakedness they clothed themselves in silence. Or come to think of it now I look back on it, maybe it was not them who had silenced us but us who had silenced them.

At last the hatch of the ticket office opened and the queue inched forward. The women searched in their purses with stiff fingers for coins to pay. Mother paid for us all and the attendant issued us with towels, stiff narrow towels, red and white.

We took off our clothes in the small cubicles that lined the sides of the cold pool and followed Mother and Veronica to the steamroom. The door was a double device of flaps of perished rubber through which you had to push. The drag and slap of rubber on wet flesh was nauseating, and the place stank. Out of the choking pall of steam bodies emerged like somnambulists, dreamily; on slatted benches bodies slumped. At first I found it unbearable, this immersion in the dripping essence of a stink so high I held my breath. And the heat! I breathed and thought my lungs would scorch. But once I was seated on a bench beside my mother, a folded towel between my bum and the steaming slats, I took example from my mother's languid smile. Her lips were parted as if she were dreaming, and her eyes were closed. I closed my eyes and smiled to be like her, I tried to dream what she was dreaming, and found myself seared by a pleasure so intense that it was the excrucation of it not the heat that sent me out of the steamroom.

Veronica was standing outside, the baby under her arm as if it were a parcel, her blonde hair falling to cover her breasts.

'Come and have a shower,' she said, in her film-star voice.

The white tiled floor was cool beneath my feet. A row of showers, open to the room, sprinkled water into a shallow trough running the length of one wall. In the corner, a burly attendant in a cap and apron was calling to Veronica. The attendant held out her scrubbed hands, patted her thighs, and laughed. Veronica dumped the baby in her lap. The attendant began to speak in Danish. I could tell from her tone of voice that she was asking Veronica a question. Veronica shook her head and stroked her smooth stomach with the flat of her hand. I looked at her and she winked at me. I knew that she was lying to the attendant – that was what the wink meant. I thought that she was pretending to be the mother of the baby. I wandered off towards the showers, bored by Veronica's game. I thought she was doing it to make me laugh, but from under the shower I saw that she was still chatting to the attendant, her arms folded maternally across her bosom. When she joined me I asked her what she was up to.

'Nothing,' she said. 'What do you mean?'

'What did you say to that woman?' I asked.

'We were talking about the freeze,' she said. 'About the fishing. Her husband is a fisherman. The dangerous weather for fishing. The men can't get the boats out.'

'What did you say about the baby?'

'She asked me how old he was and I said I couldn't remember. I said I wasn't his mother,' said Veronica.

'Oh,' I said.

Veronica's stomach was bisected from the navel to the top of her pubic hair by a streak of golden hairs. I stared at her stomach. I stared at the curls of her pubic hair.

'What are you staring at?' she asked me.

'You,' I said. 'Why? What are you going to do about it?'

'Nothing,' said Veronica, poking me between the ribs with the tip of her pointed finger. I stuck my tongue out at her. Water ran into my mouth.

There they were, the witches and widows, now divested of their clothes. They soaped themselves conscientiously under the showers, their dripping bodies veined garishly and bald.

'Don't stare, it's rude,' said Veronica.

After the shower she took me to the cold pool. My brother and sister were splashing about in the shallow end, almost unrecognisable, blue-lipped and squawking, their heads seal-like under caps of streaming hair. Veronica ran to the edge of the pool and dived in. Her long body sliced the water. My mother was climbing gingerly down the steps, hugging herself and grinning. I stood on the edge where Veronica had stood, and braced myself to dive. I saw her streak by under the water.

'Go on, let's see you dive,' said Mother.

'I can't,' I said.

I couldn't. I couldn't take that cold head-first. I wobbled on the edge.

'I can't,' I said.

Then I jumped.

It was after the first visit to the bath-house that we were introduced to the game of doctors and nurses by Klaus's daughter, a little curly-headed child of five or six who turned up one afternoon in March in the charge of an old woman called Nana, in whose honour we decided to rename the ship's cat. The ceremony took place on deck, presided over by Veronica, who had been the first to point out the similarity between the old woman and the little tabby animal with its pale green eyes and wet nose. The cat submitted to the first part of the proceedings but became alarmed when Veronica sprinkled him with water; he scratched her, leapt out of her arms, and disappeared. The adults remained on deck, tossing back glasses of the whisky that Nana had brought, while we children went below to play.

'I am a doctor,' said Sandy, Klaus's daughter. 'You be nurse,' she said to me in that special voice children adopt for games of make-believe. 'You are ill,' she said to Flora.

Louis lifted Flora up and laid her out on the big bed where Mother slept with Klaus.

'I'm going to have a look,' said Sandy, removing Flora's knickers. 'Nurse, make the patient keep still.'

Flora was beginning to struggle and cry out.

'Shut up,' I said, and slapped her on the leg.

That quietened her.

'Open your legs,' said Sandy.

Flora obeyed.

'The vagina,' said Sandy, pointing. 'Nurse, fetch some water.'

I poured out a tumbler of water from the jug beside the bed. 'Here.'

Sandy stuck the corner of her handkerchief into the water and dabbed Flora's vagina with it.

'Better?' she asked.

'Yes,' said Flora.

'All finished,' said Sandy. 'Get dressed. Now you be a doctor,' she said to me.

The game was making me uneasy.

'Go on,' said Louis.

Sandy was taking off her knickers.

'All right. I'm a doctor. You be nurse, Flora.'

'I'm nurse,' said Flora, laughing.

Sandy lay down on the big bed and we knelt round her as she opened her legs. Then we heard footsteps on the stairs, and voices.

'Quick,' I said.

As the adults entered the cabin, there we were playing innocently under the table with the cat.

'Puss puss puss,' said Flora.

'No, stupid,' said Louis. 'Nana, Nana, Nana.'

'Puss puss puss,' said Flora, refusing to use the new name.

'Vagina. Smelly vagina. You've got a vagina,' said Louis.

'Really, Louis,' said Mother. 'Please!'

When we had finished eating supper Nana went away, taking Sandy with her. That night we were allowed to have bedtime stories in the big bed with Mother and Klaus. Klaus occupied one side of the bed, and Mother the other; we were in between.

At first we wriggled and fidgeted but once the stories began we managed to settle comfortably, three clean naked children all in a row. Mother told three stories, one each, oldest first. Louis's story was a tale of bloodshed and heroism, mine a mysterious romance, and Flora's an animal fable. They all lived happily ever after. We pleaded for more but Mother was firm.

'It's late,' she said. 'It's time you were all in bed.'

'We are all in bed,' said Louis.

Flora closed her eyes and pretended to be asleep.

'I'm not tired,' I said.

'To bed,' Mother ordered.

'No,' said Louis.

I looked at Klaus with big eyes. I stroked the crisp hairs of his chest with the palm of my hand. I pressed my cheek against his cheek and whispered into his ear.

'Please,' I said. 'Go on, let us stay.'

I won him over and Mother was overruled.

'Nana left some presents for the children,' he said.

We began to bounce up and down under the covers.

'Presents, presents,' we chanted.

Klaus used the blade of his pen-knife to cut the string of a brown paper parcel. We cheered and Mother smiled resignedly. For Louis there was a sailor jersey buttoning on the shoulder and for Flora a corduroy pinafore. My present was a knitted green Tyrolean jacket, brass-buttoned, trimmed with black and red braid, the front covered in giant edelweiss.

'Try it on,' said Klaus.

The oiled wool was scratchy next to my skin.

'How pretty. Go and look in the mirror,' said Mother.

As I climbed out of bed I became aware of my big pink bum sticking out from under the peplum of the jacket and my tummy protruding out of the flapping fronts. It was the colour of my body partly and partly the fat that horrified me. The jacket only served to make me feel more exposed. And yet I did not flee from the jeers of my brother, my brother who was pointing at me and shouting 'vagina vagina' and I did not flee from my mother's howl. I stood in front of the mirror screwed to the back of the cabin door and stared at my reflection. In an attempt to relieve my shame I fastened the buttons but the jacket was cut in such a way that once fastened it transformed me; it gave me an hour-glass figure, a film-star figure, the figure of a woman. Klaus was whistling at me. I wanted to run away and throw the jacket overboard into the sea but I was held by my reflection and their eyes. I did a little dance in front of the mirror, I waggled my bum at the audience, I simpered and cooed. Then I cast about me in horror for a pair of knickers or a sheet to cover myself but there was nothing to hand so I fled.

The thaw came at the end of March; a pale sun melted the snow and streams of icy water ran in the gutters of Marstal, washing the streets clean. The whiteness of the frozen harbour sparkled in the new light and broke up; on the surface of the water remnants of the ice gleamed and dipped like the floating bellies of dead fish.

The *Selma* ran off the slips, took on board a cargo of timber, and sailed away.

The noise of the bandsaw and the shouts of men filled the harbour and the little shipyard. Whole trees, stripped of their bark and cut lengthwise into massive planks, were fed into the steamer, a forty-foot cylinder of bolted steel, to be bent into shape by the wet heat for building and repairing the hulls of ships.

The keel and ribs of a half-built schooner stood in a scaffold of timber like the ruined nave of an upturned church. Light was distilled through roped tarpaulin as through stained glass. Men in tallow-coloured aprons hung in pulleyed cradles from the top of the scaffold and hammered, their mouths full of nails.

The mate returned from his family in Hamburg and after a night of drinking in the fo'c'sle with Klaus the two men set to work. They spread out the sails and sat cross-legged on the roof of the deckhouse to mend them. They spliced ropes and oiled pulleys and scrubbed the deck on their hands and knees. They unbattened the hatches and cleared out the hold and made a fire in an oildrum on the shore.

I stood by the fire with Louis and Flora and watched the coloured paper and ribbons and dead Christmas trees burning. I saw the wings of the Christmas fairy go up in flames.

'Where are we going?' I asked Louis.

'To Finland,' he replied.

'Why?'

He did not know the answer so I asked Klaus.

'We are going to take a cargo of grain to the Finns. Three hundred tons of corn,' he said.

'Why?'

'Why why why,' he replied, poking the fire with a stick.

'Why?' I asked, in a fit of agitation, mad to be given the answer.

'Shut up. Shut it or I'll put you in the fire,' he said.

'Why?' I shouted, ducking to avoid his swipe.

'Why?' I shouted, and ran away.

I poked my tongue out at him from the safety of the deckhouse roof but he did not see me – he was looking into the fire. The mate passed below, carrying a sack of dead wood.

'Kurt, why are we going to take grain to the Finns?' I asked.

He shouted at me, 'Why not?'

On the floor of the galley I found an old paperback book, a novel without illustrations that I stuck up my jersey and carried off to my bunk. I lay in the half-darkness and examined the cover; it showed the naked belly of a woman, goosefleshed and suntanned, her waist encircled by a string of pearls. Written on her skin in pink lipstick was the word HOT. In place of her navel was a single staring eye. A chameleon was crawling across her right breast. The other was cupped in a hairy hand like a spider. The word NIGHT was printed in black across the top of her knickers. HOT NIGHT. I opened the covers and began to read. I don't know what the book was about – I know it started off on a train – but I lost interest after the first page and gave up. I stuck it back up my jersey and put it back where I had found it. Mother and Veronica came into the galley and began to peel potatoes. I sat at the table, the book on the floor at my feet. Innocently I leant over and picked it up.

'What are you reading?' said Mother.

'Oh,' I said. '*Hot Night*. Why?'

'Show me,' she said.

I showed her the cover. She looked at it for a moment in silence then snatched it from me and threw it out of the galley door overboard into the sea.

'Why can't I read it?' I asked.

'It's disgusting,' said Mother.

'Why?'

'Peel some potatoes,' said Mother, thrusting a knife into my hand. 'Don't go on.'

At supper the man began to explain to me about journeys and cargoes and making a living.

'Oh. I see,' I said. 'Now will you tell me about the book? Mummy threw a book into the sea.'

'It was learning to swim,' said Louis. 'Bum book bum book bum book,' he added.

'Ssh,' said Klaus.

'Mummy said it was disgusting,' I said.

'Some books are unsuitable for children,' said Klaus, his moist eyes smiling on me kindly.

'Unfit for anyone,' said Mother.

They began to argue.

'Why did you chuck it away?'

'Because I did.'

The man raised his voice. Mother's face was scarlet.

'Enough, woman!' Klaus looked around the cabin slowly, fixing us one by one with his big blue eyes.

'Tomorrow I am going to take the children in the lifeboat to the island.'

'A journey!' I said.

'Across the sea!' said Louis.

'And me,' said Flora.

I can't remember much about the journey except for the hunger we suffered. It was dark by the time we reached the island, dark and cold and lonely, and we had nothing to eat. Klaus held me in his arms and we slept under a tarpaulin in the boat and at dawn we searched for food. Klaus tried to stone some gulls but he missed and they flew away. I found a few sour gooseberries in a prickly bush. There was nothing on the island apart from a scorched conical building that smelt of fire and fish. Flora was crying. I tried to eat seaweed but it was bitter. I tried to eat grass but it was coarse as straw and salty. We filled our waterbottles from a little stream. The island was wind-blown and desolate so we sheltered against the flinty wall of the conical house and waited for Klaus.

'He'll find something,' said Louis.

'It might be a trick anyway. A test.'

'Chocolate,' said Flora.

'Or cheese.'

'Steak.'

'Cake.'

'Toast.'

'Peaches.'

'Custard.'

'There he is,' said Louis.

But Klaus was empty-handed.

'I want to go home,' said Flora.

'So do I.'

'So do I.'

Klaus looked out at us from beneath his fierce eyebrows. 'We're hungry,' said Louis, faintly.

'Starving.'

'Hungry? Look at you! Three little fatties. Hungry? Hungry!' he shouted.

Flora was bellowing. 'Mummy, Mummy, I want to go home.'

'So do I,' said Louis.

'So do I.'

At last Klaus relented.

'I am disappointed in you,' he said, as we climbed into the boat.

I sat in the prow and turned away from Klaus, into the wind. I did not want to see the big let-down in his face, the pained smile, the play-acting anger, the soppy look in his eyes.

Louis cast off and we sailed away.

It was late afternoon by the time the lifeboat was tied up alongside the ship. One by one we climbed up the rope ladder and ran into the galley in search of food. There was a note from Mother on the table. *Gone shopping. See you later. Love from Mummy.* Klaus made us sit round the table and wait for him to feed us. He gave us one slice of black bread and sugar each.

'Your rations,' he announced. 'Make it last. You may start.'

We ate slowly, reining in our ravenous appetites, crumb by crumb. Never have I tasted anything so delicious. I have tried black bread and sugar since in an attempt to savour again the pleasure of that afternoon, but without success; I found myself chewing on a starchy mess that served only to obscure the memory of that ecstasy.

I was skipping barefoot on the deck when the grain lorries arrived. The drivers rigged up an open chute and began to shovel grain into it. Dust rose as the grain poured out of the mouth of the chute and fell into the hold. I peered over the edge of the hatch and watched the heap of grain growing in the gloom below. Kurt joined the drivers in the back of the lorry and picked up a shovel. Dust and chaff caught in his beard as he worked. Once the hold was half-full Klaus jumped down into the sea of golden corn and waded about, spreading it evenly into the corners with an old broom.

At last the hold was full. Some of the cargo spilt onto the deck and lodged in the cracks between the boards. Klaus and Kurt battened down the hatches, anxious to keep the corn dry.

Soft splashes of warm rain watered the ship for three days and three nights while preparations were made for the journey. Cases of provisions were taken on board and two men were hired, a bosun and an old seaman who wanted a passage to Finland. The tanks were filled with fuel and water. On the morning of the fourth day the sky was blue and empty – there was nothing but blue between the ship and the sun – and for four more days we waited in the perfect sunny stillness for a wind. It was not exactly a gale that blew up in the end, more a balmy sea breeze, laden with salt and the smell of cured fish, but it was enough; we used the engine to manoeuvre out of the harbour and then the sails were set. Once the engine was turned off I felt the wind seize the ship and lift her through the waves towards the open sea. And the spilt corn had sprouted – there was a lawn growing on the deck, a lawn tender and fresh as any garden in the spring. I heard Veronica laughing. She stood in the stern of the ship by the galley steps and pointed at the lawn.

'England's green and pleasant land,' she said. 'Shall we buy a cow? Did you remember to pack the lawnmower?'

Together we walked from the stern to the bows, from the bows to the stern, port, starboard, starboard, port. Over the side there was nothing but sea. The horizon made a circle around us. You could see that the planet was round. Veronica took my hand and started to sing – 'Old MacDonald had a farm, ee aye ee aye oh.'

It was difficult to tell how long we were at sea because the days were interminable; dawn followed dusk with no more than an instant of pale night in between. I went to sleep several times after meals but it was not clear to me as I sat down at the galley table or on the deck with the crew whether the plate of potatoes and bacon or potatoes and herring that I was given was breakfast or lunch or supper.

The salt spray and wind caught in my hair and matted it. I liked to wear it loose, parted in the centre and hanging down my back, but the agony of having the knots picked out made me submit to a new style, somehow more ship-shape – pigtails. The ends of the plaits were fastened with strips of coloured cloth out of the engine rags. I felt a bashful pride in my new appearance, in my emergence from behind the curtain of my hair, and when I skipped on deck with my new ball-bearing rope I thought I was sweet.

Apart from skipping, and writing a page a day in my diary, I spent much of that journey peeling potatoes. Klaus used to come to me as I sat with my bucket and knife on the steps of the galley and inspect the thickness of the skins.

We had a potato-eating competition, Louis and I, and he beat me, twenty-one to seventeen. After that I went to bed in my clothes, too tired to undress, and had a dream that I was in a little round boat with Klaus, turning round and round in a poster-coloured sea. I woke up and scrambled up the steps and saw that we were moored on a jetty by a pine forest. Finland! Everyone was asleep apart from me. I leapt down the gangplank and hopscotched on the shore. Finland was a white and sparkling country. I realised that the whiteness was frost. We had sailed back to winter. My bare feet were freezing. I hopped across the snow.

It was a tall house we used to live in, before we went to sea. There were two men in the room, and Mother was pouring tea out of a white pot. My father was smoking a cigar, the laces of his boots were undone, the bunch of keys on his belt jangled. The other man was blond, blond like sheaths of wheat, like butter, like driftwood. I was wearing my new party dress, a mass of pink and yellow flowers, I was sitting in the big blue armchair, waiting for my nails to dry, waving my hands in the air, kicking my feet up to admire my new shoes (Harrods patent leather, grosgrain bows), I was five, my feet did not reach the floor. Who was that big blond man? My father slipped out of the door.

'Come and sit on my knee,' said the man. 'My name is Klaus.'

'Be careful of my nails,' I said, as he grabbed me and lifted me onto his lap. He gave me some sweets and a ten-shilling note. That won me over. I thought he was kind.

'Where's Dad?' I asked.

'He's gone,' said Mother.

Klaus was playing with my hair. I liked him. He was tall and blond like the man in *The Man from Uncle*.

When I was three I bit off my tongue. The doctor sewed it on again. When I was four I fell out of a sportscar as it took a corner and landed on my finger. I had to have seventeen stitches. The bone is set rigid and the nailbed is injured. When I was ten I broke my finger again. I fell over in the road and screamed until my mother came and carried me into the back of an ambulance. When I was twenty I got headbutted in the face outside a pub in Archway and broke my nose. When I was twenty-one I had a haemorrhage following an abortion and lost two pints of blood.

Finland was cold, Norway was lush, Sweden was clean, Germany was boring, Poland sent out an armed guard and would not allow us to disembark. In Hamburg after several months of service the bosun and his mate got fed up and deserted, taking with them some cold meat and Danish cheese out of the galley and setting off when everyone was asleep. They bad-mouthed us in the docks, spreading the word that Klaus was a playboy sea-captain and couldn't pay his crew. We were unable to find replacements for them – the jobs were advertised by word of mouth in the harbour bars but there were no applicants. We had to return to Marstal two men short.

After a day or so at sea Klaus decided to turn Louis into a sailor. He taught him how to splice the frayed ends of ropes together, how to use the big brass compass mounted on its pillar by the wheel, how to read charts and take the helm. The beginning of the journey was uneventful because the sea was calm. Louis stood at the wheel on an upturned crate, a small proud smile on his face. Every few minutes he checked the compass reading to make sure the ship was on course. The charts were spread out on a chest beside him.

The bilge pump broke down at dusk of the fifth day, but we weren't shipping much water, so Klaus and Kurt went on working in the engine room, repairing some leaking fuel-feed pipes with wire and rags. When they tested the engine in preparation for the docking at Marstal there was a fuel blowback that caused a small explosion, the flames of which Klaus managed to smother with a blanket.

We approached the coast of Denmark as it got dark. The wind began to blow quite fiercely. Klaus and Kurt abandoned the engine and descended into the hold to fix the bilge pump, because we were beginning to ship water a little faster.

In the main cabin Mother was feeding Conrad at her breast and I was playing cards with Flora. Klaus could be heard running on deck, shouting. He opened the hatch to the stairs and shouted at Mother to get up on deck. Mother gave the baby to me to hold and ran. Conrad screwed up his face in disappointment at the interruption of his feed but I stuck my little finger into his mouth and that kept him quiet.

Flora and I stationed ourselves in the deckhouse so we could see what was going on. I held the baby in my arms and peered out of the window. Mother was trying to keep hold of a length of rope attached to the jib. The force of the wind was so strong the rope was burning the skin off her hands. She let go of it, the sail began to whip through the air, and Klaus started screaming at her. Then the wind changed direction and the main boom swung across the ship, creaking as its speed increased. Mother shouted at Klaus to duck but he was too slow; the boom whacked him on the back of his head and knocked him off his feet. I began to laugh but Flora was crying and then I began to cry. In the gloom I saw Klaus get up off the deck and wipe tears out of his eyes with his sleeve.

Mother was hanging onto a rope that was dangling out of the rigging, the sleeves of her jersey pulled down to protect her hands. As the ship went about for the third time she was lifted off her feet. I couldn't work out what was happening. Louis was shouting and waving on his box by the wheel. I left Flora in the deckhouse and went to see why he was shouting. I found him nursing bruised and bleeding knuckles; the wheel was spinning so fast the spokes had lashed his hands. Together we tried to catch hold of it as it spun but it was too painful, and so we waited for Klaus, smiling at each other in anticipation of his fury. Kurt appeared wearing gloves and lassoed the wheel with a strong cord.

The wind was pushing the ship backwards towards a pair of lights bobbing in the distance. The men fought to lower the sails, but it was too late – we were suddenly so close to the dock that we could smell the human smells drifting across the water; fried food, laundry, the warm smell of shore life.

Klaus went below to try and start the engine up again. We heard the wheezing of the starter motor and then nothing. The gap between the stern of the ship and the shore was narrow, narrowing. The mainsail was unfurled and flapping all over the deck. A freak gust of wind filled the trapped jib and blew us backwards past a narrow jetty where the pale hull of a moored sloop could be seen glistening in the dark sea. The stern of our ship hit something black protruding from the dock. I fell over and Louis fell on top of me. There was a sickening crash and the prolonged splintering noise of wood breaking up. The impact crushed the lifeboat. Klaus emerged from below into the darkness and tripped over my foot. Louis and I were giggling on the deck. Klaus hauled us to our feet, held us one in each hand by the hair, and knocked our heads together. The pain made me puke up onto Klaus's boots. He was swearing in German.

'*Hundsvotze, hundsvotze, hundsvotze.*'

Mother managed to lower the jib while Klaus and Kurt tied up the ship and got the bilge pump working. The next day Conrad fell overboard and floated on his back with his arms above his head until his absence was noticed and Mother and Klaus and Kurt and Veronica dived in and saved him. We spent several weeks in the dock while the baby's inflamed chest and infected lungs confined him to his bed. The doctor diagnosed pneumonia. Klaus bartered two hundred Camel cigarettes and a litre of schnapps for a large bottle of penicillin. A Finnish engineer spent a fortnight overhauling the engine in return for a passage to Finland and Louis burned the remains of the lifeboat on the shore. We took on more crew but the lifeboat was not replaced.

I know that the first hot country we sailed to was Spain, but I can't remember anything about it apart from the donkey rides. On the way the sea was rough; it was not a dirty sea like the Baltic in a storm, a sea of chopping slapping waves and spray that made you spew up your breakfast; this was different – the sails were lowered, the boom was lashed, and we had to wear lifejackets. The sea towered above us like a green mountain, a glassy mountain rearing out of the valley in which we floundered, its sides trembling as they heaved towards the sky. The ship dived, lurching lower and lower into the black empty cave of the storm. There was a deathly moment of stillness before the mountain fell. The crash thundered through the ship and the deck was awash; I felt we should never rise again out of that swallowing sea. I was pop-eyed and empty. I was waiting for my whole life to pass by in front of my eyes like a film. Mother was holding my hand. I heard rattling as if the keel of the ship were scraping the sea-bed but at the point when I abandoned hope the ship began to surge up out of the water. We rose higher and higher until we towered above the storm on the peak of the mountain. I heard Klaus laughing, there was silence, and then we fell.

Louis and Flora were braver than I. I left the galley and went below to lie on my bunk, to groan in the half-light, to submit to the storm, and to weep. Saliva dribbled out of my mouth and wet the pillow in which my face nestled, and I sank, spinning into an oblivion of nausea, under my heap of blankets, held in my own embrace, round and round. I sank quite calmly – the pull was irresistible – I let myself go. Darkness, a dusty bandage, tightened round my head, black velvet, blinding me. Soon I would reach the pit of my sickness and there I would rest while the storm raged. It was then that the storm tossed me out of my bunk. I banged my head on the floor and had to go up on deck to vomit. Veronica held onto me as I leaned over the gunwale and retched but nothing came out of my mouth. The fresh air made me feel better. I scrambled along the wet deck on my hands and knees, making for a little cubby-hole built under the masthead. I wedged myself into the heap of tangled rope and folded canvas it contained, and from the safety of this vantage point I settled down to watch the storm. Mother found Louis and Flora hanging on the rope swing Kurt had rigged up on a line slung between two masts. Water was streaming off them; each time the ship rolled they swung out over the side on the end of their rope and were dipped shrieking into the sea. Mother staggered on the deck, and screamed. She made them join me in my little cupboard.

'It's boring in here with her,' said Louis.

'Anyway, it's my house,' I said.

'You stink,' he replied.

So we sailed into the heat. We were going to Trinidad, emigrating, to start a new life in the Tropics, to bask in the sun and be free. The heat was so intense and unremitting that Klaus let us sleep on deck. I lay on my back under the magnificent sky until I was overwhelmed by sparkling constellations, the inky canopy, and the moon.

I turned over onto my front, listening to Mother singing a lullaby. She must have been singing to me because Louis and Flora were asleep – I could hear their even breathing. Then Klaus came and kissed me goodnight. His lips nuzzled in my hair and on his breath I smelt the manly smell of tobacco and schnapps. I peeped out from under the tarpaulin that covered me and looked into his mournful eyes.

'Sweet dreams,' he said.

Mother set up a schoolroom in the deckhouse, and gave us lessons, sums and spelling, so we would not get left behind. Once the journey was underway there was not much to do. Kurt and Veronica lay on top of the hatches all day long, stroking each other and drinking beer. In the evening we all ate together in the galley or the main cabin, then the men got drunk. Sometimes they sang sea-shanties, swaying from side to side and stamping their feet, but mainly they played cards late into the night. Mother sewed by the light of the oil lamp and told us stories. Veronica was unable to settle. She would sit on Kurt's knee, smoking a cigarette and sipping out of his glass, laughing when he lost a hand, laughing when he touched her breast or thigh absently, his eyes averted; or she would stand beside Klaus, her hand on his shoulder, and pour him a drink. Then she would go up on deck, you could hear her pacing about up there in the dark, until Mother sent one of us to fetch her. One night I found her in my cubby-hole, her moonlit face luminous and shadowed like a skull. I saw that her cheeks were wet – she had been crying. I asked her why.

'Never you mind,' she said, and took my hand. She squeezed my hand so hard it hurt. 'Ask no questions, hear no lies,' she said.

That was the only time I ever saw Veronica cry. When Kurt shouted at her she shouted back or turned away, her face set against him, and laughed. When Klaus dropped a mallet on her foot she hopped up and down for a minute, her eyes and mouth puckered in pain, then she smiled. When Mother gave her dirty looks, looks that would have made me weep, she returned them, making Mother lower her eyes and sigh. Once I saw her naked in the main cabin, when Klaus and Mother were up on deck, studying her long brown body in the mirror. Her face was blurred with tenderness, the pink tip of her tongue visible between wet lips. I watched her but she did not see me, and I slipped away.

There were palm trees in Madeira, dried and dusty, casting stunted shadows on the little squares of bleached grass that grew at intervals along the sea-front. We sat under a sunshade in the middle of a neat park and drank Coca-Cola. In the distance we could see the masts of our ship, still and slender against the blue sky. Mother took us to a little shop on top of a hill and bought Flora and me some dainty mats as souvenirs. There was no dusk – night fell suddenly, and the men spent the night ashore. Mother and Veronica sat up in the main cabin and talked about them. I kept quiet in my corner; perhaps they did not notice me – I was not sent to bed. I heard Mother sigh and mutter, sigh and curse. Veronica shrugged her shoulders.

'A cow, her udders,' I heard her say. 'Sorry,' she added, grinning.

The effort to understand made me fidget.

'Rose, get to bed,' said Mother.

Veronica was painting her mouth as if in preparation for a night on the town.

'Let me have some,' I said.

Veronica made up my face like a woman but I wiped it off.

'Isn't Veronica beautiful?' I said, looking at Mother to measure her reaction. 'Beautiful,' I repeated.

'Go to bed,' said Mother, and I went.

In the nets dragging the sea behind the ship we caught big ugly fish that Mother fried to feed us. My brother pointed out to me the flying-fish flashing out of the water like knives. I was struck by the tropical glamour of that unlikely species, half bird, half fish, the mystery of it, their flashy ways.

For days on end we didn't see any ships – we saw nothing but the sea, the endless sea, the fish, sea-birds, and the sun. At night I felt the vastness of the invisible ocean, and by day the smallness of the ship confined me.

After six weeks at sea we put in at an island port off the coast of South America. I had almost forgotten how to walk on dry land and so when we went ashore I swung my arms like the sailors in their bright uniforms who strolled in the town. I saw the tourists look at us, at the peeling paint of our ship, our engine-rag outfits, at Veronica's legs. The people of that little port hung onto Klaus's hands. He was an impressive sight, six foot six and blond, wearing a pale suit; they were after his money. At the time I thought they took him for a god. I wondered what they thought of me.

Next day I woke up in another port. I was proud of my nautical life. I swaggered in that filthy part of the world where the sun bred life out of every pool of water, every fallen fruit or broken bone. The heat overcame me. I wanted to swim in the sea but as I picked my way down to the foaming water across the margin of sand dropping away from the side of the melted road I looked down at my legs and my sandalled feet and saw that they were infested by small black biting insects, feasting on my blood.

The third place we stopped at was even hotter. Klaus hired a car and drove us inland to an historic village. The main street was derelict, almost deserted, the windows of the squat buildings shuttered with cardboard against the noon sun. I heard the crunch of the armour of cockroaches, breaking up under my feet, followed by the wet sound of their spilt insides pressed between the sole of my shoe and the pavement. A man poured petrol out of a blue metal jug onto the road, clearing a path for himself through the cockroaches – his feet were bare. Rats grazed in the gutter and on the heaps of refuse piled up outside the closed doors of a mobile drinks kiosk parked outside a painted chapel. Klaus told us that it was siesta time and made us get back into the car.

In the port a liner docked to take on fresh water. The passengers disembarked for the afternoon, parading in their whites outside the Grand Hotel. A man drew his knife in a street fight but Mother covered my eyes.

It makes me dizzy, short of breath and dizzy, with the sickness of one who no longer travels, to hear the names of places we called at towards the end of that journey dropped into the chatter that surrounds me as I lean over the bar of the Warwick Castle, waving a five-pound note; for me those places exist only as memories of my childhood, in the past buried in my head.

Guadeloupe, Martinique, Puerto Rico, Venezuela.

I am unable to separate those island harbours and coastal towns one from the other in the muddled geography of my memory. I hear them introduced into the conversation and it is as if I am witness to an exhumation. I cannot conceive of those hot ports of my past still floating, at the end of a seven-hour flight, under the terrible sun.

I was nine when we arrived in Trinidad. It was the rainy season. Klaus settled us into a house in the suburbs of Port of Spain and rented a television. Mother hired a black maid called Eva to help her manage. Eva taught her how to make banana fritters, and sang romantic songs.

The house was made of polished stone, solidly built and modern, its bare walls on the inside almost cool to the touch. I shared a bedroom with Flora, where we slept together in a double bed, as far away from each other as possible, under a mosquito net.

Louis shared a bed with Conrad, who was now nearly two years old. Eva dressed the baby up in a little straw hat, sat him on the veranda, and gave him an old saucepan to play with.

Green tree-frogs lived in the lavatory cistern and giant moths the size of tea-plates landed on the television screen, attracted by the light. Spiders with pincers like crab-claws crawled across the ceiling and lizards basked on the window-ledges. I caught a lizard by the tail and it ran away, leaving its tail in my hand. In the yard I watched a mongoose kill a snake.

The small bananas that grew at the back of the house were called figs. The oranges were green. We ate cassava root that Eva dug up out of the earth, and boiled plantains, and rice. A yard boy came by once a week to scythe the prickly grass. Klaus paid him one penny and Mother gave him a drink of water.

At first the mosquitoes devoured us and the bites festered, making it painful to walk. But once we had got the hang of keeping our skin covered in the evenings and smothering ourselves in insect repellent, the bites began to heal. After that we suffered from boils on our thighs and buttocks. It was impossible to walk. I sat on the veranda in the shade, making an embroidered picture for Klaus on a square of white cotton salvaged by Eva to use as a duster from a worn-out sheet. The picture showed a yellow cottage surrounded by roses and hollyhocks, under a pale blue sky. When it was finished I took it into the bedroom where Klaus was lying naked on the bed under a sheet and I gave it to him. He took me into the bed with him and kissed me on the lips. He folded my little sweaty body in his arms and breathed loudly in my ear. My nightdress rode up to my armpits and I felt the hairs on his heaving chest scratching my neck and stomach. It was hot in his embrace, hot and dark and safe, and it meant that he loved me. Mother came out of the bathroom adjoining their bedroom wrapped in a white towel and shouted at him. He shoved me out of the bed and I ran from the room into the sitting room and turned on the television but it was only the testcard on all channels.

Then Klaus took us to a party on a big white sloop called *Dreamboat*. Once all the guests were on board the boat set sail and sped across the water, her white sails dazzling me. Out of a system of loudspeakers rigged up on the mast a man's voice poured – Groove me baby, make me feel good inside. Oily bodies pressed together, grinding, limbs entwined. Veronica and Kurt were dancing in the middle of the deck. Veronica took off her shirt and swung her breasts in time to the music. Her nipples jiggled in the sunshine, blurred, pink as flowers. Kurt leaned over her, his hanging tongue curled at the tip, and she popped one of her nipples into his mouth. He sucked on it, his eyes closing, gently, like the eyes of a baby. Men circled round them, clapping and yelling, and my vision was obscured.

Black men in white jackets bowed and grinned and served drinks. Klaus did not much like the island people – he said they were liars, bad sailors and cheats. He called them niggers. He threw one of them overboard into the sea and laughed as he watched the man flounder and grope for the lifebelt someone had tossed after him.

Louis was eating watermelon; he held the smiling black-toothed slice in both hands and buried his face in the scarlet flesh like a kiss.

Mother was wearing a faded sleeveless pinafore dress, knee length, made out of dark brown cotton, the pattern of yellow ochre irises too large, like curtain material. Mother was not dancing. She stood with her back to the dancers, the baby asleep on a heap of cushions at her feet, and leant over the side, Flora's hand in hers. They were looking at the silvery coast that was disappearing slowly, and the sea.

'Rose, come here,' she called.

'Why?' I asked, taking the hand she held out to me.

I knew what she wanted. She wanted her daughters to stand by her, to hold her hands and show the men who looked at her and the glamorous women who made her feel bad that she was a mother. She wanted us to make her inviolable.

'Look at Klaus,' said Flora.

Klaus was dancing with Veronica, his hands clasped behind her back, the tips of her breasts brushing his chest as she swayed. His hands slipped apart and scurried across her back. I watched them crawl from her waist to her buttocks and fasten there. Klaus's knuckles whitened. I saw him jam his knee between Veronica's legs. Her face was dreamy, her lips parted, the tip of her tongue visible, and her pretty teeth.

'Look at the shark,' said Mother, pointing out to sea.

In the distance a black fin was gliding through the smooth water, leaving a small white wake.

'Louis,' she called. 'Come here.'

Louis ambled over, eating a piece of barbequed chicken.

'Watch the kids for me. Look at the shark,' she said.

Mother was trying to distract our attention. Obediently we turned our backs on the dancers and looked at the fin of the shark cutting through the water. Mother walked away from us towards the dancers. The lure of the dance was irresistible. Louis was the first to turn back, then I. Flora followed, jumping up and down and shrieking. She shrieked and pissed herself.

'Look! Look!'

At first I thought Mother and Veronica were having a cuddle, rolling about in each other's arms on the deck, but then I saw Veronica's bared teeth and blood pouring out of her nose. She was holding onto a handful of Mother's hair, yanking Mother's head up by the hair, dropping it onto the deck. I screamed and tried to run but Louis held onto me and told me to shut up.

'Save her, Louis,' I said.

Louis was looking over the sea at the shark.

'Look at the shark,' he said.

I leaned against the gunwale and watched Mother slapping Veronica. The palms of her hands were smeared with blood. Then someone poured a bucket of water over the fighting women, dousing them down as if they were dogs. Kurt appeared out of the crowd and stooped beside Mother, offering her his hand. Mother raised her dripping head helplessly from the deck and let it fall again. I heard a gasp as Klaus drew his knife, and then there was silence. Kurt began to back off. As he retreated he tripped over Veronica's foot and fell on top of her. Klaus waited for him to get up, his face monstrous, purple. Veronica laughed. Kurt turned to look and Klaus caught him by the ear. Klaus raised the blade slowly and sliced the earlobe away from Kurt's head. He held the earlobe between finger and thumb, examined it, then threw it overboard into the sea.

THE CURSE

The heat built up from scorching dawn to high noon, when I feared the sun. The sun would strike you down. I took shelter on the veranda and idled away the shimmering afternoon until the rain came. It rained each day at four. I stripped off on the back porch and stood naked in the deluge, the swollen raindrops pelting me. The rain was warm as tears, a magnificent respite from the afternoon sun that never failed to lay me out. I tilted back my head and let the rain fall into my mouth. The water tasted rich like milk or blood. It ran down my throat, slaked my thirst, and fell into my open eyes. The pleasure of the drenching rain was intensified by my knowledge that it would end abruptly, leaving me to steam.

The rain stopped falling. My footprints evaporated instantly behind me as I crossed the back porch; that was the evidence disappearing -- no evidence of my pleasure remained apart from the banging of blood in my ears and the fact that I was weak at the knees. I leant against the side of the sink at the back of the porch and steadied myself. The white china of the sink was cool. The brass tap was mottled and dull. Out of the plughole rose the homely smell of bleach. On the draining board some washing was steeping in an enamel basin and a washboard hung from a nail in the wall. The clothes I had been wearing lay in a small pile at my feet. I looked at them as if from a great distance. My mother had bought me the shorts from the market at Port of Spain. The knickers were dark green, old school knickers from England when I used to go to school. My name was written in indelible ink on a piece of tape sewn across the back of the waist. The sleeveless blouse was finished in bias binding round the neck and armholes, and fastened at the back with little ties. The material was fading, the orange flowers turning brown. I heard the hoarse croak of a bullfrog from behind the coconut tree. It sounded like a man bellowing. I got dressed and traipsed about in the yard until my hair was dry.

Then I heard my mother calling me.

'Rose. Rose darling. Cooee.'

It sounded as if she were playing some childish game, hide and seek, coming ready or not, and it irritated me, her sing-song voice, the way her voice drove solemn thoughts out of my head. After my shower I liked to kick about by the shed, in the shade of the coconut tree, to survey the dripping dreary yard that was our territory, where the frogs belched in puddles of rainwater – I wanted to be by myself. Mother was waving to me from the back porch, waving a blue exercise book at me, my coffin-shaped pencil case tucked under her arm.

'Come on. English Vocabulary. Time for schoolwork. Let's be having you,' she said.

I sat on the veranda chewing my pencil, the exercise book open on my knee. My mother set me a task. I had to think of as many alternatives as possible for the word 'nice'. I wrote NICE in capital letters at the top of the blank page and tried to think. I tried to overcome the desire to scribble all over the blank page. I looked at my thighs sticking out of the legs of my shorts. The chewed pencil tasted of paint and wood. A car passed by on the glistening road.

'Come on,' said Mother, over my shoulder. 'Think.'

I could think of nothing.

'Go away,' I said.

Mother tutted at me and went away into the kitchen. Perhaps I had not understood the question. There were no words that meant nice except nice. What was the point? It was because Mother thought that the word nice was inexpressive, unimaginative, weak. She wanted me to increase the size of my vocabulary. She had given me a little red book in which to write new words. The book was called Vocabulary. It is a nice book. I am a nice person. You have a nice face. Mother came back onto the veranda and put a glass of lemonade down beside me on the floor. That was nice. The word filled my head and excluded all others.

'Say thank you,' said Mother.

'Thank you,' I said.

'How are you getting on? Shall I give you a clue?' she asked.

'Yes please.'

Mother smiled at me.

'Lovely. Kind. Pleasant. Pretty. Delicious. Attractive. Fun. Interesting. Decorative. Festive. Delightful.' She took a breath.

'Go on, now you think of one,' she said.

The list made me angry. I could think of nothing nice.

'No,' I said.

Klaus went away on the ship to take cargoes from island to island. Mother said that we could not go with him because it was too dangerous, so we stayed in the house. Twice a week we went to the beach. The taxi boys called for us in two cars, bashed-up family saloons that rattled in the road in front of our house, the first a malevolent brown colour, hand-painted, emitting puffs of white smoke, the back windscreen missing, a shower of broken glass scattered on the floor, and behind, a black Ford, low and broad, glossy like the wing-case of a beetle, a radio strapped under the dashboard with Elastoplast. There were four boys, I can't remember their names, three of them rode in the brown car with Louis, out in front; I used to watch them sharing bottled soft drinks and flicking their cigarette ends out of the windows as we followed along behind, Mother, Flora, the baby and I, driven by the oldest, a fat boy wearing mirrored shades who drove at a sedate pace and tuned the radio to receive a broadcast of the World Service, presumably in our honour. I liked to hear the bells of Big Ben. I asked him if he liked swimming.

'I can't swim,' he said.

The road wound round and round the mountain, rising a little higher each time until the air was thin and we could see clouds below us. The cars stopped when we reached the top so we could admire the view, and then we began to descend, round and round, I thought at first we were retracing the route of our ascent, I couldn't really see the point, but as we reached the bottom of the mountain I realised we were on the other side of the island, and before us, deserted except for a few dogs, the hot white beach and the sea.

The taxi boys parked the cars in the shade of a couple of palm trees, opened all the doors, found music on the radio, and settled down for an afternoon dozing in the sun.

I had grown out of my swimming costume so I wore a pair of my old school knickers for swimming. I wrapped myself in a towel and got undressed inside it like Mother did, in case the taxi boys were looking at us. Mother stretched out on a rug and rubbed oil into her skin.

'Be careful,' she said, as I ran into the sea.

The waves were large. I swam out a little way, then rode the surf on my stomach, letting the waves carry me. I swam out again, further this time, and rode back, blissfully. Swimming out for the third time I saw a big wave moving in, rising and swelling as it approached, rearing out of the water, green and angry white against the blue of the sky. I thought it would break on my head and kill me, I waited for it, but it did not break; it lifted me until I bobbed above the beach, shrieking like a sea-bird and waving at Mother below me, held high by the power of the water. When the wave dropped me I fell through the air into a trough of white water. The impact split my legs open and hit me between the thighs. I opened my eyes in agony, saw the bright water around me, and sank. I was ground on the sea-bed, waiting under the weight of water, held on the bottom by the sucking of the sea. At last the sea let me go and I rose to the surface, I was washed up on the beach, winded, the sea had stripped me of my knickers and taken them away. The skin of my stomach was flayed red and smarting. I crawled back into the shallows because I did not want the taxi boys to see me naked, and shouted to my mother for a towel. She helped me out of the water and lay me down beside her on the sand to rest. Once I had got my breath back I put my shorts on and went back into the sea.

Once a week we went to market in Port of Spain. After the taxi boys had driven us home, Mother invited them into the house for a cold drink. They refused to come into the house, but sat on the veranda, drinking Mother's home-made lemonade. I was sad to see them drive away because I liked them. I liked the smell of their cigarettes and I liked the glamour of their blackness. After they had gone I felt empty. Then it rained.

I was standing inside the gate of our yard looking out at the puddles in the road when a man came out of the house opposite wearing a beige safari jacket, his oily hair blue-black like a bird on his head. He waved at me and I waved back. Then he crossed the road and put his hand in his pocket. I saw the gleam of coins in the palm he held out to me, the gleam of his brilliant teeth and the gold hanging round his neck like a rope. To encourage me he nodded and smiled. I was wearing a sleeveless blouse, I wanted his money, I felt naked.

'Go on, big girl,' he said.

I took a couple of coins and watched him slide the rest back into his pocket.

'See you,' he said, and I waved as he opened the door of a big black car and slid into it, disappearing behind smoked glass. For my birthday he bought me a new blouse, black embroidery on brown, but it did not fit me. It was too small so I gave it to my sister.

A boy found a deadly coral snake coiled on a slab of smooth concrete by the side of the road. Men gathered out there as night fell and I was afraid of their voices. They closed in on the snake, silently, armed with cutlasses and cleft sticks. The boy prodded the snake with a long bamboo but it did not move because it was dead. One of the men saw me watching from the veranda.

'Hey, white woman,' he said to me. 'Come and feel up snake.'

I ran across our yard, climbed over the gate, and knelt at the man's feet. The snake was black and red in the light of his torch.

'Feel it,' said the man.

I held out my hand. The snake was warm.

'Do you want it?' said the man.

'What?' I asked.

'The snake.'

'Yes,' I said.

The man cut the snake with the blade of a small knife and peeled off the skin.

'For you,' he said, holding it out to me.

I took the skin, thanked him, and ran away.

In the morning the taxi boys came back. They were sitting in the black car outside our house, the brown car parked behind. I went into the kitchen to tell Mother.

'What do they want?' she said.

'I don't know. Go and see.'

'You go and see.'

'Come with me.'

Together we walked out to the cars.

'Hello,' said Mother.

'Come with me,' said the fat boy. 'Come and see my family.'

I got into the back of the brown car. The fat boy followed me. Mother went to fetch the other children. Wild music was playing on the radio of the black car as we set off.

The taxi boys lived in a big shack. Chickens scratched in the yard and a white goat, tethered to a stump, was drinking water out of a tin plate. In the dappled light of shady trees the family of the taxi boys came out to greet us. There were twenty-six of them, I counted, smiling and holding out their hands. They gave us lovely food to eat, fried fish and plantain, callaloo, and mangoes warm from the tree. At first I thought that the three women whose heads were tied up in big scarves were the mothers or aunts of the taxi boys because they were so womanly, offering us dishes of chicken wings and Johnny cakes, pouring punch into spotted beakers, but then I realised that they were hardly more than children, they were the young wives of the taxi boys, their own children playing in the yard. The mother of the taxi boys kissed me and held me in her arms like a baby. She smelt of chocolate. Her mother was dozing in a hammock strung between two trees. Two old men were playing dominoes on an upturned oildrum. A generator hummed in the shade of a golfing umbrella, and beside it, under an awning of corrugated iron that stuck out from the roof of the shack, a big wooden radiogram was belting out a hymn. A silver car without wheels rested on chocks of oily wood, the boot and bonnet open, a pair of thin legs protruding from underneath. A group of young girls gathered round us, touching my skin and hair solemnly, kissing Flora and the baby. In the doorway of the shack a man in a cowboy hat was staring at Mother. Behind him other men could be seen peering over his shoulders out of the dim interior into the sunshine.

'Where is your man gone?' the man said. 'When will your man come?'

'He's gone to sea,' said Mother, blushing as if she feared that he would never return.

The man laughed. Mother amused him with the bird-like tilt of her head, her eyelids lowered to hide her big grey eyes, the modesty of her gestures, her lovely smile. I reached out for her hand and held it in mine. The man was cruel. I knew that from the threshold of his home in the midst of his family he was poking fun at Mother's manlessness.

In the evenings we sat in front of the television, Louis on one side of the sofa, me on the other, and Mother in the middle, with Flora on her knee. By the flickering light of the television I read the illustrated *Iliad* and *Odyssey* Mother had had sent out from London in a parcel of educational books. When I got bored I would ask her to tell me a story.

'Tell us about when you were a little girl,' I said.

On the piano at my grandfather's mansion flat near Baker Street I had seen a photograph of my mother as a child wearing a pinafore and black button boots.

'A long long time ago before I was born when my mother was no more than a tiny child with golden ringlets framing her elfin face and a little cap of green velvet decorated with garlands of leaves and berries perched on her head like a pixie and Queen Victoria sat on the throne of England and ruled her subjects with a will of iron my mother's family made a fortune in saucepans,' said Mother. 'I spent the summers with Uncle Bee and Uncle Ron, my mother's bachelor brothers, who lived together like lords on a large estate in Shropshire, hunting and shooting and collecting animals and birds from far and wide to bring home as pets. Fearsome bullocks the size of baby elephants and wild boar with tusks as sharp as knitting needles roamed wild in the wild park surrounding their house. If you were chased by a crane you had to climb up a tree to save yourself. It was supposed to be character-forming, to make you brave. It was only on horseback that I felt safe, out of the reach of the savage beasts who loved little girls. It was very very scary. Once when I was riding with my sister in the park I fell off my darling pony and hurt my arm. I lay in the long grass, my ear to the ground, and heard a terrifying rumbling noise. It was the thunder of hooves. The bullocks were coming to get me. I curled up and pretended to be dead. The panting beasts pawed the ground and snorted at me. My sister galloped away in an attempt to distract their attention but they did not follow her. I was left alone amongst them. I kept quite still and shut my eyes and tried to disappear into the earth. It was my pony that saved me. When I heard the rubbery vibration of his lips and smelt his lovely warm smell I began to sob as if my heart would break. He had come to rescue me. My arm was too sore to remount, the pain made me weak, so I walked by his side to safety. I loved my pony more than anything else in all the world. The bullocks raised their mournful eyes and moved away from the patch of crushed grass where I had fallen.'

'More! More!' we begged and pleaded.

And so Mother went on. 'My mother spent much of her time in bed, drinking tea and suffering with her nerves. Under a heap of pelts of gazelles shot in the plains of Africa by her father she propped herself up with a mountain of cushions and read magazines in the half light. The curtains in her room were closed across the high windows that looked out onto a formal garden of mazes and arbours because she could not bear the greenness seeping through the windowpanes – the green light hurt her poor eyes. Whenever she ventured out in daylight she wore a funny little visor on her forehead made out of stiff brown cardboard, fastened behind her ears with knicker elastic, because she thought that sunglasses were rather vulgar. The curtains of her bedroom were only opened at night. She would rise after dark like a witch and stand at her window in a long white nightgown, looking out at the stars and the moon. I never saw her at the window myself, but the housekeeper, who had to go up to Mamma's room every night after dinner to discuss the menus for the next day, took me into her confidence. She said Mamma was like a ghost standing there in her bare feet, gazing at the moon. I was afraid she might catch her death of cold and die.' Mother took a breath.

'Did she die?' I asked.

'No, no, that was later on, when I was grown up,' said Mother.

'Anyway,' she continued, 'before I was born the cook got into a scrape after a dance held in the village to celebrate the end of harvest. Mamma said that the cook was drunk, or under the influence, as she called it. Mamma told me that as a consequence of the cook's inebriation a situation developed. She said the woman was defenceless because she was sadly wanting in the morals department and as a result a hired hand took advantage of her innocence and left her in the lurch with a child. The man could not be traced. Mamma allowed the child to be brought up in the kitchens. She slept in the corner in a packing case beside the boxes of onions and carrots and potatoes. Mamma regarded this charitable act as a great kindness to the cook, and considered the cook to be forever beholden to her. The child's name was Florence. When she was old enough Mamma trained her as a lady's maid. She brought Mamma her tea in bed, washed Mamma's silk underwear herself in a basin in the bedroom, sang as she ironed the sprigged petticoats and smoothed the frills of the little camisoles, and spent hours brushing Mamma's hair. A bed was made up in Mamma's dressing room so Florence was always near in the night if Mamma rang the bell beside her bed. Florence spent all day at Mamma's side, listening to her going on and on about the past, her unhappiness, and love. Mamma liked to talk about love. Somehow Florence managed to encourage Mamma to rise in the afternoons and go for a walk. I used to watch them in the gardens, Mamma leaning on Florence's arm, bending to sniff at an opening rose, resting on a bench in the shade of a blossoming tree. Mamma said she owed her health to Florence, she owed everything to Florence. Then one night Florence did not come home. Mamma was distraught. She wept and my father had to call in the doctor to administer a sedative. Florence returned in the morning, hand in hand with a groom from the neighbouring estate, who had come to ask for her hand in marriage. Mamma sent him away. Then she summoned Florence to her bedside, and Florence helped her to dress. Got up to the nines in coffee-coloured silk with a corsage of rosebuds on her bosom, she went to see the groom's master, Lord Burcott, and used all her wiles to convince the old gentleman that he must somehow get rid of his groom. Lord Burcott kissed her hand and acquiesced. The groom was told that Florence had died mysteriously in the night. Lord Burcott, well known in the vicinity for his humane methods with servants and tenants, sent the miserable boy to train as a gamekeeper at his Highland hunting lodge, "to get the benefit of a change of air". Mamma returned in triumph and told Florence that her man had run away. Florence confessed that she was pregnant. Mamma told her that she had been left in the lurch, just like her mother, who had died of her sins. Florence got down on her knees and begged Mamma to spare her, to let her stay. Mamma told her to get up off the floor and go and wash her face. Florence's child was stillborn. Grief made Florence pale. Arm in arm with Mamma she tottered about the garden, shedding bitter tears. Then one day Mamma lost a diamond ring, accused Florence of theft, and threw her out of the house. Florence had to go to the workhouse. Mamma took to her bed again. A week or so later she found the ring in the folds of her bedjacket. She wept for the loneliness of her life without Florence but could not bring herself to admit to her mistake.'

'She was wicked,' said Louis.

'Or mad,' I said.

We sat quietly for a moment, looking at Mother.

'Is it true?' I asked.

'Yes,' said Mother.

'More,' said Flora.

So Mother went on. 'My upbringing was a formal affair, probably very similar to that of my mother – for the best part of the day we were forbidden to leave the nursery, because that was where we belonged. We only saw our parents once a day, my brother and sister and I. A succession of nurserymaids, none of whom stayed in the house for more than a year, prepared us for this audience. Each had her own methods. The first one I remember was Molly, who scrubbed our faces with a cold facecloth to bring the colour to our cheeks, and burnt my hair ribbons in the nursery fire as a charm against vanity. The next was called Susan, a great fat lump with hair horribly yellow like butter, who called us "poor children, my poor little ones", and kissed us over and over again on the lips. These nurserymaids lived in fear of Miss Dilly, the governess, as we did ourselves. Their job was to make us clean so that we would pass Miss Dilly's inspection. During the inspection, the poor girls used to quake with fear. Then they would be dismissed not knowing whether we had passed or failed. The governess would decide at her leisure whether or not to punish the nurserymaids. Sometimes she discussed it with us. Other times she was cruelly silent as she buttoned us into our clean pinafores and arranged our hair with her own fair hands. Then she would deliver the verdict. "Susan will have to be burnt a little," she would say. Or "Molly is spared." We accepted her verdict in silence. If we were dirty, Miss Dilly would hold the fingers of the offending nurserymaid in the nursery fire until she screamed. She said that cleanliness was next to godliness. The nursery fire stood for a taste of hell to come, she said. If our noses were snotty, the governess would pinch the upper arm of the nurserymaid until it was black and blue. She was not allowed to smack us, so she took her fury out on the nurserymaids and invented subtler tortures for my brother and sister and me. After the inspection Miss Dilly took us to see Mamma and Papa, who received us either in the drawing room or in Mamma's bedroom, depending on the state of Mamma's health. One wet dark afternoon Uncle Bee and Uncle Ron came over for tea. Miss Dilly lined us up outside the drawing room and opened the door. Mamma was wearing a lilac dress and Papa was standing by the fire, smoking a cigar. The governess curtsied four times, first before Papa, sinking deeply as if she wanted to kiss his polished boots or throw herself on the floor at his feet, then before my uncles, bobbing neatly, holding out her skirt like a little girl, and last before Mamma. The last curtsey was abrupt, no more than a little nod of the head and the smallest possible bend of the knees – Miss Dilly despised Mamma, and took no trouble to hide her feelings. Mamma graciously invited the horrible woman to join the party for tea. This was an honour for Miss Dilly, who after all was only a servant, for all her airs and graces. She sat beside me on the sofa, and suffocated me with the naphthalene smell floating out of the folds of her costume. Papa gave us some cake. Uncle Ron and Uncle Bee were telling rude stories. Uncle Ron had seen his nanny's knickers hanging on the washing line. Uncle Bee had seen his nanny peeing in the nursery sink. Mamma said to be careful in front of the children and tittered behind her hand. Then I told a story. I said that I had peeped through the keyhole of my mother's bedroom and seen my father naked by the bed, naked from behind. Saying the word "behind" made me laugh. No one else was laughing. Mamma gasped and dropped her teacup onto the floor. I turned to Papa, hoping to see him smile. He was tight-lipped and scarlet, incredulous, scandalised. The governess hauled me out of my seat and dragged me out of the room by the hair. She put me on a diet of bread and water for three days and made me sleep on my own in a passage. In the night Mamma floated out of her room and I screamed because I thought she was a ghost. She took pity on me and let me sleep in her bed but in the morning she made me get up and go back to my blanket on the floor so that the governess would find me there when she got up.'

'Oh, you poor thing,' I said, looking at my dark brown dusty feet. 'How terrible.'

'It wasn't so bad,' said Mother.

Flora began to cry. Mother began another story to cheer her up.

'Guess what?'

'What?' said Flora, and sniffed, wiping her nose on her sleeve.

'When I came to London it was such a relief not to have Miss Dilly breathing down my neck that I didn't clean my teeth for two years.'

'Naughty naughty,' said Flora.

I rose and cooled my forehead against the wall that divided the sitting room from the bedroom where Mother slept with Klaus. The England in Mother's stories was a remote place. It was not the England we had left behind us. From the tropical heat of our new home I found the England of Mother's childhood even more alluring than the England I had known myself. I somehow managed to overlook the cruelty so plainly described in her stories and thought only of ponies and cooks and nurserymaids, figures to which I was sentimentally drawn because of the life they hinted at. It was a world I knew I did not belong to, a world from which my mother had disassociated herself or had come to feel excluded. Out of these stories I try to piece together an understanding of her past.

Mother lay in her little bed and pressed her face into the sodden pillow, her tears releasing from the ticking and goose feathers a mildewed birdy smell. From her mother's bedroom she could hear cries, regular moans of pain, deep sucking breaths, the rhythmic groan of bedsprings, a short silence, laughter, the tinkling cascade of glassware and china breaking up, the aching thud of a body falling onto a carpeted floor, her father's furious voice shouting bitch, you bitch, you bitch.

On an outing to the seaside at Brighton in 1951 my mother began to bleed while swimming in the sea. She waded out of the water and stood shivering on the pebbles in her knitted bathing suit, the blood running down her thighs. People began to stare. Mother looked down at herself to see what they were staring at and screamed when she saw the blood. Miss Dilly wrapped her in a towel and laid her down on the floor of the bathing hut.

'It's the curse,' said Miss Dilly.

Mother thought that she was dying. She closed her eyes and kept very still. The governess peeled off Mother's wet bathing suit and fastened a sanitary belt round her waist.

'Pull yourself together, dear,' she said. 'It happens to all of us.'

Miss Dilly stuck a sanitary towel between Mother's legs. It was soft and cosy, cosy like a nappy, healing like a bandage on a wound.

'Now you are a woman, a fully-fledged woman,' said Miss Dilly.

'Am I wounded?' said Mother.

After that Miss Dilly powdered Mother's hands every night before she turned out the light.

'Keep them on the counterpane,' she instructed. 'That will stop you from enjoying yourself.'

Mother was woken up every morning by the hand inspection. Miss Dilly would kneel by the side of the bed and examine the hands of her charge for smears.

When my mother was twenty-one she got pregnant and went down to the country to tell her mother. She was accompanied by her older sister, also pregnant, who was married and living in Oxfordshire.

'Congratulations,' said my grandmother, when she was told that her oldest daughter was expecting a baby.

'Darling,' she said to my mother, 'I don't remember you having been married.'

My mother warned us about her father, when we stayed with him and his new young wife in Scotland, after his retirement – she told us he was rather partial to little girls.

I stand at the window of my room and think of my mother. The traffic on the Westway sounds like the roar of the sea. It is September. Lying face-up in a cardboard box on the pavement below me there is a calendar, one of those red and black ones, the full moon represented by a white disc, the new moon a crescent on red. A man stops to pick up the calendar, examines it, and throws it away. Another man passes, stops to pick up the calendar, hesitates, and throws it away. The bug-eyed head of a plastic doll is sticking out of a rubbish bin. A woman stops, lifts the doll out of the bin, wraps it tenderly in a piece of cloth, and lies it down in her basket as if to sleep.

Last night I dreamt I had a baby. I put it upstairs to sleep in a double bed. I kept on pretending to the people who were milling about on the landing and staircase that I had forgotten about the baby – I wanted to appear casual, unconcerned.

And yesterday I had one of those terrible arguments that terminate in weeping. My boyfriend closed the front door and I was alone in the hall, sobbing like a child. I shed the tears that connect the present to the past, not by a process of comparison, but directly, by feeling. That door closing on me wiped out twenty-five years of my life. I was three again, the front door slammed and Mother was outside with suitcases and a man. I howled. The au pair girl took me upstairs and scrubbed me down with a flannel in a bath of disinfectant until I was scarlet and then she cut off all my hair.

I always wanted a pet, something cuddly to call my own, a baby fish that I could nurture, or a pony, like most little girls, so I could look into its eyes. After the tropical rain had fallen on that fecund island the puddles in the pockmarked road were full of frogspawn that hatched out quickly in the heat of the sun. I caught some tadpoles in a jam jar and made them a little pond in a Tupperware box on the back porch. I filled the box with rainwater so they would feel at home, and gave them small pieces of bread and dead insects to eat in case they were hungry, even though Mother told me that tadpoles consumed the nourishment in their own tails. My tadpoles grew legs and their eyes became bulbous but their tails were not disappearing. I put a stone in the water to make an island for them in the hope that they would be encouraged to climb out onto it but they did not. I had to take the stone out again because it took up too much room; the tadpoles were enormous, side by side in their own slime. I willed them to grow up, to consume their own tails and hop away, but they would not. Week after week I stared at my pets in their box until the thought of what I had done to them became unendurable and Mother took them away.

Klaus came back in the middle of the night, head-banging and calling my name.

'Rose, Rose.'

The thud of his forehead on the stone wall outside my room was a sound I recognised. I did not answer his call. I hid under the sheet and kept very still, pretending to be asleep. I could hear his breathing and smell his breath. He was not banging his head hard enough to crack it open. The violence was measured, and it was his cowardice that frightened me. It was his cowardice that made him want me when he was maudlin drunk in the middle of the night. He was weak. I knew that he was trying to resist the lure of my plump little body. And I wanted to be loved. The dull thud of his head on the stone wall made me ache. It made me sick. I heard him enter my room. He was calling my name. Under the sheet I crossed my legs and tried not to piss myself. It did not occur to me to scream. I knew that Klaus was unhappy. I did not want to see his soppy eyes that hurt me and messed me up because they said too much, they were asking too much. I pretended to be dead until he went away.

At Christmas we made a Christmas tree out of the dried branch of a palm tree and decorated it with silver paper. Klaus sent us a card from Jamaica, a glittering picture of Mary and Jesus, and Mother balanced it on top of the telly. I deciphered the lopsided scrawl of his message inside the card – Barbaric custom adoration Greetings lonely Klaus. The message made me wince. I asked my mother whether it was us or Klaus who was lonely.

'Not lonely, silly, lovely,' she said.

Was it us or Klaus who was lovely? It was a lie anyway. Mother said it was us, we were the lovely ones. She said he must have been drunk when he wrote it. I wanted to send him a card but we did not have his address. I made Eva a purse out of a scrap of material and wrote her name across the flap in felt-tipped pen. She gave us some cakes sprinkled with coloured sugar-strands. It was Christmas but we wore shorts because it was so hot. We watched telly because it was so boring hanging about in the heat with nothing to do.

I went for a walk once with Louis and watched the vultures circling above the shanty town, waiting for a death. Black children stood about by the side of the road on spindly legs, their stomachs distended. A black man touched my hair and ran away.

'Let's go home,' said Louis.

He took my hand and we ran.

At the end of January on the way back from the beach Mother told the taxi boys we would no longer be needing them. They sulked, assuming she was displeased, and the fat boy, who was driving, reduced the speed of the car until it moved forward as slowly as a hearse. It was as if he wanted to prolong forever the last journey. In the end Mother was forced by the uncomfortable silence in the car to explain that it was a question of finance.

'We are a little down on our luck, that's all,' she said. 'Please don't take it to heart. As soon as things look up, we'll get in touch,' she said.

The boys were bashful, too respectful, as if anxious to avoid any possible suspicion that they were taking advantage of our poverty, the drop in Mother's social position. They offered to take us over the mountain free of charge.

'No offence meant, Missus,' said the fat boy. 'For the children,' he added.

'I couldn't possibly accept such a generous offer,' said Mother. 'The petrol,' she said. 'Think of it! To think of the expense we'd be putting you to!'

The fat boy was grinning with embarrassment. After that we didn't go to the beach any more.

We finished up the last of the sacks of good rice that Klaus had bought in bulk in Port of Spain and had to make do with the stinking stuff that they sold by the pound out of a drum in the forecourt of the garage. Eva stayed on for no pay. She showed Mother how to dig up the root of the cassava tree and boil it to eat. The leaves of the tree were affected by a damp blight, yellow and orange, and then it died, keeling over in the night.

The grass in the yard grew long and sharp because the yard boy didn't come any more to scythe it with his cutlass. I loitered in the shade of the back porch and watched the ants march in single file along the raised concrete path that led to the shed. The ants carried leaves and twigs many times their own size. I wanted to interfere with them, because the order and determination of their lives annoyed me. I wanted to halt their progress or change the direction of their journey, to make them take fright and drop their loads. I dropped scraps of paper in their path. The ants picked up the scraps and carried them off. This pleased me.

Klaus came back in March, bringing with him large bottles of Coca-Cola and packets of salted nuts in an airline holdall. He sat naked outside the door of my room, waiting on a wooden chair. When I came out of my room he took me on his knee and pulled off my nightdress. I was happy. I thought it meant he loved me. He wanted to fuck me. Then he went away. We received a postcard from him a week or so later.

'Ship sunk. Go home. Klaus.'

THE COUGH

The ship we sailed home in was called the *Ipinia*, an Italian passenger liner crewed by flamboyant suntanned sailors, their white uniforms decorated with gold frogging and epaulettes like fancy-dress costumes, their eyes black and handsome in the shadow of their caps.

Tourist-class passengers slept in dormitory cabins deep below the surface of the sea. We shared ours with three men from St Vincent who were sailing to England to find work. The air in the cabin was dank and cool like a cave. Canaries hung in cages in the corridors, as a safety measure; if they fell off their perches it was a warning; the oxygen level was dangerously low. The washrooms were open-plan and windowless, lit by lightbulbs hanging on brown wires from the low vaulted ceiling. Along one wall a row of bathtubs stood on little feet opposite a line of spectacular basins, capacious and ornamental, as if salvaged from some grand hotel. The lavatory cubicles were built without doors. Black women were treading washing in the bathtubs, squeezing it in the fancy basins, spreading it out on the tiled floors and scrubbing it, wringing it out and hanging it from makeshift lines strung up between the light fittings. When the weather was stormy, women vomited into the bathtubs and lay about on the floor, rolling their eyes and moaning. Water splashed out of the basins and lavatory bowls. The floor was awash with watery vomit and broken pieces of shit in brown water.

In the tourist-class dining room a vast reproduction of Picasso's *Guernica* decorated one of the walls. The room was a corridor that led from the kitchens to the rest of the ship, containing one long table, flanked on either side by benches. The passengers sat huddled together and watched as waiters in duck-egg blue jackets danced past carrying above their heads silver platters of swans and castles made out of sculpted and dyed mashed potato. In front of each person was an empty metal bowl and spoon. A woman with big arms came out of the kitchen carrying a galvanised bucket on her hip from which she slopped out ladlefuls of gruel-like soup or yellow stew. An Indian man who was sitting next to me puked up into his bowl when he smelt the steam rising from his meal. Mother gave us seasickness pills each morning containing antihistamine that induced in me a dullness making mealtimes endurable.

The tourist-class swimming bath was made out of a stitched bag of oiled canvas suspended inside a hole in the deck. The pool was full of green seawater, the sides railed with lengths of sodden rope looping through eyelets of salt-corroded metal. It was situated in the shade of the ship's funnels so the water was cool and the sides were coated with patches of slime and crusted salt. Flora loved to splash about in the water, wearing a school regulation swimming costume in bright blue nylon. I was hanging onto the rope at the edge absently watching the bright blueness ripple and shimmer under the water when I realised that her head was fully submerged, she was sinking, sideways, her pink thighs flailing, a dreamlike motion dragging her down. I considered letting her sink, never to be seen again, her fat little bum bumping once or twice before settling for good on the bottom, but I could not. I swam out to save her but she fought me, tearing at my slippery skin with her nails. I shouted at her to keep still but she could not hear me. I tried to kick her in the head and knock her out under the water partly in fury that she had hurt me and partly so that I could save her but I missed and my foot landed on her chest, making her sink even deeper. In the end I dived down under the water and managed to get a grip on the straps of her swimming costume. I dragged her to the edge of the pool and hauled her to the surface. She gasped and wailed through blue lips.

'I saved your life,' I said. 'You should be thankful.' I felt hateful towards her when I saw the red weals of her nails on my arms and chest.

At night when I could not sleep in that cabin full of breathed air I would wake Louis, dress in the dark, and escape with him up the narrow stairs leading to the tourist-class deck, holding my breath as we pressed ourselves to the walls of long corridors where strange voices could be heard from behind the studded metal cabin doors, breathing out as we chased across abandoned recreation rooms, the table-tennis tables illuminated by the pale glow of the emergency lighting, whispering as we passed the locked-up bar, smelling the fumes of stale alcohol emanating from under the door. The stairs to the second-class deck were less narrow, and carpeted with deep-pile carpet, the fibres of which were matted together and felt warm like the pelt of a dog on the soles of my feet. To get to the first-class deck we had to run the whole length of the ship, through the empty lounge where the entertainments officer organised games of bingo in the afternoons, over a locked wrought-iron gate hung with a sign in several languages, past the barber's shop with its blue light winking on and off in the window, along a glass-screened observation deck and under a red rope slung between two brass posts. That brought us to the foot of the stairs. Before us the sweeping steps were palatial, shallow and battened with polished brass rods, the carpet a good rich claret red. We climbed the stairs slowly, the pile velvety between our toes, and came out in the ballroom, under chandeliers. The french windows at the far end of the ballroom opened onto the deck reserved for first-class passengers, a paved courtyard with pillared recesses and bushes of eucalyptus growing out of blue urns, where marble dolphins spouted into a mosaic pool. We dived in, drinking in the forbidden water, fresh water, black as the night.

I made friends with the barber's son, Giovanni, a boy who sucked parma violet cachous to make his breath sweet and nurtured a crop of fine black whiskers on his upper lip. In a storm he led me by the hand to the ballroom where the furniture was lashed to the walls with rope and showed me how to ride on the grand piano. He took off the brakes and as the ship lurched the piano careered across the ballroom, sliding on the polished floor until it crashed into the far wall, sounding a melancholy chord. Giovanni put the brakes back on, looked solemnly into my eyes and kissed me on the lips, prickling me with his whiskers.

When we arrived in England I had to take medicine every night because I developed a terrible cough. The medicine was yellowish, a pastel yellow that was threaded, when unshaken, by strands of pellucid orange. The pharmacist gave me a supply of transparent spoons with which to feed myself. The cough was not one of those racking boneshakers that produce blood; my cough was unproductive. I felt as if the air around my bed floated with little fibres and microbes that crept into my chest. I tried breathing through a corner of my sheet in the hope of sieving out the irritating particles but this was ineffective; the sheet itself harboured microbes in its weave. The fact that I had been instructed by my school teacher to commit to memory the multiplication table up to twelve times twelve and the Lord's Prayer by the end of the week did not help. And if I coughed too loudly Louis would wake up and shout at me to shut up. The cough was dry and hollow, insistent, distressing. The cough distressed my mother and I tried to stifle it in my pillow. Our Father which art in heaven hallowed be thy name. I ran the words through my head. The teacher had written them out for me on a little square of cardboard I kept by my bed. The times table I had to construct for myself. The teacher said that I was intelligent and that she could see no reason why I should not be able to work it out using a process of addition and common sense. I tried for several successive nights to figure it out as I lay coughing in my bed. The patterns of the numbers appeared and disappeared. It occurred to me that the answer to seven times nine was the same as the answer to nine times seven, but to find the answer to nine times seven I would have to begin again with once seven is seven and work my way up. Then I would finish the seven times table, having forgotten where I was, and find myself repeating yet again the eight times table. I seldom found my way to twelve times twelve. And as for the Lord's Prayer the words meant nothing to me. Thy will be done on earth. The words were dreary and unpoetic. I muttered them as I lay coughing in my bed but they did not console me. I was not praying. I did not believe in God.

The test was on Friday. By Thursday night the cough was worse. The medicine was bitter and soapy; it made me retch. What nauseated me was the flavour of scent and sugar that had been added to the medicine to mask its real nature, to make it taste better. I thought perhaps the orange strands held this foul flavour in their pellucid brightness so I tried to drink the medicine without shaking it. I poured myself a spoonful of the yellow liquid, leaving the orange strands in the bottle, but it tasted just the same. I had the whole of the Lord's Prayer by heart and as for the tables I was word perfect. On Friday afternoon the teacher gave me a gold star in my test book. On Friday night I was still coughing.

There were four beds in our room, one each for Louis, Flora and me, and one for Mother and Conrad. A sink was plumbed in under the back window between a three-ringed stove and a tabletop fridge on a drop-leaf table made of yellow formica. At bedtime Mother kissed us goodnight, turned off the lamp beside her bed, backed into the kitchen, and closed the folding doors that divided the room in half. Through the crack between the doors I saw a yellow line of light. I heard Mother washing dishes, slopping laundry out of a bucket into the sink, opening and shutting the fridge. When I coughed Mother paused in her work to listen to me. I coughed again into the silence she made by keeping still. I don't know what happened to Klaus after the shipwreck. He disappeared. Sometimes I heard Mother crying at night in her bed but I did not miss Klaus myself.

Yes I do cry in my bed at night sometimes as my Mother did.

About that boyfriend of mine, the one who made me weep in the hall. We really are very civilised together now we have parted, after three years of clinging together, he and I; we go out to dinner together, now and then, and at the end of the evening we allow ourselves one chaste kiss then part, because we are just good friends. I do shout at him sometimes, it's true, because he gets on my nerves, but not very often. This friendly arrangement suits us both. And at night when I have read myself into a stupor of tiredness it is the rearrangement of the pillows before I go to sleep that reminds me of him – he used to be fussy about which pillow he laid his head on. His pillow makes me weep.

Before we split up we went to the country together to stay with friends. He was driving the blue Cortina, my car, and I was sitting next to him, drinking vodka out of the bottle, because journeys make me insecure. I took a tranquilliser as we passed through Southall, to make me feel more comfortable. Bangra music buzzed out of a take-away curry shop, and my boy-friend stopped the car to buy some onion bhaji. I tried on a pair of silver high-heeled sandals in the shop next door, but they did not have the ones I wanted in my size. We were taking the long route, the scenic route out of London, because I do not like the motorway. I always feel ill on journeys. He said not to worry he would look after me and that made me feel a bit better. By the time we reached Henley-on-Thames I was a little more relaxed. Slumped in my seat I looked out of the window and saw women in their headscarves moving along the neat pavement, my head level with their hips. Then we were in the country. I saw fields and hedges, cows and trees.

We arrived after lunch. There were already two cars parked outside the house, gleaming side by side on the gravel. I took several deep breaths to steady myself before opening the car door. I was bewildered by the stillness. Out of a grey bed of low herbs that grew among mottled rocks rose spikes of old lavender, oiling the soft air with their fragrance. We took a paved path leading to a bank of silvery acanthus and climbed a flight of mossy steps. There was a game of croquet in progress on the croquet lawn. The players looked up from their game to wave and our hostess came towards us across the sparkling grass in a yellow dress.

'I hope you had a good journey,' she said.

'Oh yes,' I replied. 'Fine, thank you.'

'Would you like to play croquet? We're just about to begin a new game. Have you had lunch?' she asked.

'Let's play croquet. I'm not at all hungry,' I said.

'Yes,' said my boyfriend, leaping across the lawn towards a pile of mallets that lay in the shade of a tree. He was wearing the tartan trousers I had bought him for Christmas.

'Here,' he said, waving a mallet at me.

As I ambled across the grass I watched him greeting the other guests, practising his stroke, bending to tie a shoelace. By the time I reached the tree all the players were assembled beside it, ready to begin. I kissed them one by one. Lucy, Debbie, Celia, Angus, and Cerith in his Comme des Garçons suit, the buttons winking in the sun like eyes. Cerith and I spent much of the croquet game stuck under that tree because we were unable to get through the first hoop. He offered me a cigarette. It gave me pleasure blowing smoke into the pure air. My boyfriend played a ruthless game but was knocked onto the post before he had made the last hoop. Lucy was the winner.

'Shall we have a drink?' she asked.

We sat on the grass and drank champagne. I laid my head down in my boyfriend's lap and looked up at the sky. I had to close my eyes because I could not take its endless blueness. My boyfriend held my hand. That enabled me to open one eye.

At midnight Cerith suggested that we should go for a midnight swim. The night was a soft substance; its balmy blackness blotted out the stars. My boyfriend stepped out of the patch of light that surrounded the house and I caught on to him as he waded into the darkness. I felt the bodies of the other guests beside me and behind me. We slipped blindly into the corridor of clipped trees leading to the pool and Celia began to laugh. I felt the brush of a departing heel on my shin and breath on the back of my neck.

We undressed by the pool. I did not bring my swimming costume with me and so I wore an old pair of knickers and an aertex vest of my boyfriend's, a makeshift outfit that made me feel naked. We stood round the pool in the faint light of the moon that shone through a bank of cloud and on the count of three we jumped in. The cold made me scream. My breasts were floating out of the gaping armholes of the vest. My boyfriend was groping me under the water. We exchanged watery kisses and he tweaked my nipples in the dark. His thigh was warm between mine. Then he swam away. I remembered that I had heard Cerith's breathless voice from the other side of the pool just before we had jumped.

'My whole life has been a prelude to this moment,' he said.

The house was built round a courtyard and this arrangement confused me. I found it impossible to get straight in my head the layout of the house and grounds. I never discovered where the pool was in relation to the tennis court. I could not find my way from the vegetable garden to the croquet lawn. I was lost. I don't know what prevented me from finding my bearings. Perhaps it was my nerves obliterating my sense of direction. By Sunday I was suffering from a pain in my stomach and had to go upstairs to lie down. I was miserable. It made me miserable to be such a miserable traveller. I began to cry. Once I got going I could not stop. I cried quietly but I wanted to holler and bellow. In the end my boyfriend came upstairs and sat beside me on the bed.

'Don't cry, darling,' he said. 'It makes me feel so sad when you cry. Please don't cry. It makes me want to cry.'

I looked up at him. His eyes were shiny. He was threatening to cry. It was a trick to stop me crying. I wanted to headbutt him. Then it worked. I stopped crying so that I could comfort him. I stopped crying to make him happy.

'My baby,' I said.

I held him to my chest like a child. He was smiling at me, his eyes closed, because he did not want to see the expression on my face. Hand in hand we went downstairs to lunch.

In the afternoon Angus and Cerith took me for a walk round the circumference of the grounds. We followed a muddy path that led through nettles and brambles to a wooden bridge where we stopped to spit into the black stream. We came upon a field of Herefords behind barbed wire and fed them handfuls of grass. They pressed together behind the fence to look at us with their friendly eyes and we gave them names. There were thirty or forty of the big brown-and-white animals jostling and huddled behind the fence, bullocks and cows together; we sighed at the pretty little ones and gasped at the bravado of the bullies. They were so pleased to see us, eager to eat the handfuls of grass we offered them, showing us their yellow teeth, lowing, mounting each other playfully. I ran the length of the field, calling to them, and they followed me on their side of the fence, lumbering through the mud. Cerith and Angus chased them from behind. I stopped at the far corner of the field by a coppice of rustling beech and waited for the Herefords to gather together again. They pressed their necks and hefty flanks against the barbed wire to be close to us. It was like falling in love.

When I arrived back in the dark streets of my home, under dirty rain, the majestic din of the steel bands rehearsing for Carnival wiping out the roar of the Westway, I saw that I would have to leave my boyfriend, or that he would have to leave me.

What a relief it was to be back in England, away from that tropical heat and the man. My father came to visit us, parking his Bentley outside the house in which we lived, the money rattling in his pockets as he took the stairs two at a time, and slid his hand between my mother's thighs. It disgusted me, the change in her voice when my father was around; her voice became flutey like birdsong, soft like a caress. He took Flora and me to Wheeler's, where we ate oysters, lobster, and raspberries. I wondered whether, if I ate nothing, he would give me the money to take home to my mother, but I did not dare to ask.

The house we lived in was owned by my mother, one of a pair of houses she had bought in 1962 with money left to her on the death of her mother. One house, the one we had lived in when we were very small, had been sold, when Mother met Klaus, to buy the ship and go to sea. The other had been let out room by room. This was the house we lived in now – number 17 Lonsdale Square, Islington – in the double room on the ground floor made vacant by a tenant moving on. In a cupboard under the stairs this person had left behind a pair of thigh-high boots, a long blonde wig and a heap of lurid paperbacks that I devoured.

The other rooms were occupied by a collection of people I found more alluring by far than the whispering tight-lipped schoolgirls in knee-socks strolling arm in arm round the playground of my new school, or the gangs of boys who loitered by the toilets, one or two of the ugliest of whom might deign to stoop and look up your skirt.

On the top floor in two low rooms under the roof lived a couple called Brian and Mary, and their baby Catherine, a fat dark-haired child who was endowed with eyelashes like an advertisement and seemed somehow more of a proper baby, in her pink matinee jacket and frilly waterproof, than the funny little ones my mother gave birth to. They fed the child on tins of Heinz babyfood, a method of feeding that seemed to me altogether more opulent and formal than mashing up some ordinary food with a fork or grinding it to a paste in a food mill. I was impressed by all the things that Mary bought – the packets of sterilised cotton wool, the pink bottles of baby lotion, the tubes of cream, the powder, oil, shampoo, and special soap. They had a small cupboard screwed to the wall that contained only baby things – rusks, cereals, tins, medicines, nappies, and folded clothes, some still in their cellophane packets. It was the amount of money spent and the fact that Mary had bought so many of the new products I had seen advertised on the telly that impressed me.

I would bolt the supper of pasta that Mother offered us, swallowing along with the mouthfuls of noodle and tomato my mother's apologies for the food and my anger at her for our poverty, then go upstairs to see what I could get from Mary and Brian. I used to sit with them in their little crowded sitting room and plead with them silently to give me something – anything – to take downstairs with me. About once a week Mary would give in and offer me a present; a tin of apple purée, a pair of outgrown bootees for my doll, a ribbon, a rusk. These things I would cherish as representations of a richer life, keeping them in a little basket under a handkerchief on the shelf above my bed. In the end the food always proved too tempting; the lure of present pleasure overcame my instinct to hoard, and I would give in to it. I once kept a tin of Junior Lamb Dinner for five weeks, constantly aware in the back of my mind of its presence in my basket, before warming it in a saucepan of boiling water and feeding it to myself with a plastic spoon. When it was all gone I felt a sense of loss, washed out the empty tin, and kept it under my bed. Sometimes I would wait for hours in that room under the roof and leave only when I heard my mother calling me to go to bed, defeated, guilty, empty-handed.

A Jamaican called Reggie lived in a room on the third floor at the back of the house with his girlfriend, a redhead called Nancy who weighed nineteen stone. The sight of them from the rear, mounting the stairs in single file, Nancy's wild buttocks shimmering in swathes of lamé, her legs pillars of pale flesh rising out of dainty shoes, and Reggie behind her, swinging inside a loose suit, his arms dangling, made me want to shriek. If Nancy slipped and fell on her man she would kill him.

After they had moved out and their room had been converted into a bathroom I used to lie in the tub and picture the room as it had been. Although of course I knew that the bath had not been there then, I saw them trying to squeeze into it together, their exciting bodies pressed together, the old purple smell of violet pomade and violet powder clashing with the red of Nancy's hair, the water splashing out onto the floor.

Nancy and Reggie fascinated me; I connected them in my mind with the facts of life. It was not Mother's version they reminded me of (when two people love each other they have a special kind of cuddle and then a baby begins to grow in the lady's tummy), nor the version described to us by the school nurse, who sent the boys out of the room so she could tell us frankly without embarrassment about monthly cycles and rubber prophylactics, acne and the male member, illustrating her ideas with the help of a pair of plastic dolls whose stuffed satin internal organs unravelled out of their hollow abdomens like strings of sausages in shades of pink, red and brown. No, they fascinated me with the same uneasy thrill to be had from Barbie and Ken, listening to the whispers in the school playground – 'Twas on the good ship Venus/By god you should have seen us/The figurehead lay nude in bed/Sucking the captain's penis', from watching the boys in set six to which I belonged wanking under the table when the teacher read us a story on Friday afternoons, his peachy cheek decorated with an unforgettable mole, his lovely warm voice raised to a squeak when he came to the girl's voice in the passages of dialogue, from watching Adam French snogging with Lillian Burbage, hearing the fair-haired twins in my class describe what it was like on your holidays at the seaside, on a Greek island paradise, to go for a joyride in the water on a man's penis (the man was called Marmaduke), the sound of bedsprings, the sight of my father's white bottom humping in Mother's bed, Mother's teeth bared as if in pain, the longing I felt for a boy in a pink blazer who sometimes collected his little sister from my school if his term had ended before ours. Before they moved out it was all I could do to stop myself from picturing them at it as I lay in my bed listening to Nancy's little yelps and Reggie's deep happy laughter reaching me from underneath.

Room by room the house became more or less vacant and we spread out until I had my own room, the same room I used to sit in with Mary and Brian and their baby. I painted one of the walls orange and my father gave me a miniature orange tree that I put on the table by the window. I picked one of the fruits but it was dry inside the oily skin, and bitter. The leaves of the tree turned yellow and died because I did not look after it properly. I sat at the table by the window and wrote poetry. I made a book of poems for my mother's birthday. One of the poems was about a rabbit. My mother said the poems were feeble. I read a book about a family of children who buried their mother in the garden when she died.

Several men and one or two women used to visit our house regularly, looking for a bed for the night or a hot bath or a meal or love; they were not quite guests, in that they always arrived uninvited and were not particularly welcome (not to me anyway), but I suppose now that they were my mother's friends. Most of them were nutcases, ponces, beggars, outcasts, drunks and hopeless cases. They came singly, never in groups or pairs, the better to slip into the family (they were all thin), to pass unnoticed amongst us, just one more mouth to feed. I can remember all their names, their crazy faces, voices, ways; but I will spare them. Except one, a man called Sandal, who drove Mother so mad that she emptied the rubbish bucket over his head. Even then he lingered before leaving, eggshells and onion skins stuck in his hair. Mother was made to seem stronger by the weakness of the hopeless cases; beside them she was heroic, she felt heroic.

I used to watch the big girls playing two-balls against the back wall of the playground by the wire-netting fence, juggling so dextrously, their hands cupped like tulips, the balls shooting out at the wall miraculously, one after the other, as if there were three or four of them hidden inside the folded petals of their hands. My first attempts were unsuccessful. I managed to make the balls leave my hands, hit the wall, and return, but gracelessly, without the adept stylish rhythm of the girls who would sooner die than take my arm and whisper confidences into my ear or invite me to their homes. I learnt the songs that went with two-balls – 'Each peach pear plum apple juice and bubble gum' and 'My captain went to sea chop knee to see what he could see chop knee' with all the appropriate actions, and spent every lunch-hour and playtime working on my technique. My palms smelt of rubber. Then I got the hang of it and by doing so felt forever separated from the inept, the gangling and the mad. It was a female skill I had acquired, and I was soon to pick up the variations – the low long-distance looping version, practised by Maxine Sullivan, the only girl in the school who had started her periods, and the glamorous one-hander, casual and fast, a speciality of Sally Damerell, wearer of immaculate white cardigans, the girl who started a fashion in our school for black wet-look knee-socks, an item of legwear that was worn with matching shoes to give the impression of impossibly expensive knee-boots.

At the end of the first term I had a fight with the dinner lady's daughter because she took the piss out of my red shoes. I ripped the inside of her mouth with my nails and pulled out a handful of her hair. Her mother the dinner lady took me up to see the headmistress. I looked at my hands and noticed under my fingernails drying brown deposits of the girl's blood and whitish pieces of skin. I was given a warning and sent home for the rest of the day. The headmistress said I would be spared any further punishment because I was a new girl and the dinner lady's daughter was two years older than me.

One day as I returned from school I saw the midwife's bicycle chained up to the railings outside our house. I recognised it immediately and understood what it meant – my mum was having another baby. The midwife asked me to put a kettle on to boil. I tried to go into the room where Mother was lying on her bed waiting for the baby to come out but the midwife would not let me. I had to wait downstairs with the others in the ground-floor room that had been rented out to a woman called Marigold and her daughter Moon. Marigold gave us some bread and jam to eat. I could hear Mother screaming. Then I heard the new baby cry out. I hurried upstairs carrying the kettle of boiled water and gave it to the midwife. I saw her holding the baby up by its feet. It was smeared with blood and mucus.

'It's a girl,' said the midwife.

'Let's see,' said Mother, her voice breathy and weak.

'Hang on a minute,' said the midwife, wiping the baby with swabs of cotton wool. She wrapped the baby in a square of white material.

'There we are,' she said, and handed it to Mother.

'Let's call her Sarah,' said Mother.

I can't remember what happened after that.

From my pillow I could see the moon, a whey-coloured sliver shining through the old flawed glass of the casement window in the timbered wall opposite my bed. I was reading by moonlight and by the light of a torch that was fading as the batteries died. Beards of horsehair sprouted between laths of grey wood in the hole in the wall above my bed. Fragments of plaster adhered to the hairs and dropped dust on my head. Flora was whining on the landing outside my room.

'Let me in,' she said. 'Let me sleep in your bed.'

I ignored her. I could hear her bare feet rasping on the floorboards. She was knocking gingerly on my door. She began to whimper.

'Fuck off,' I said. 'Leave me alone.'

'I'm telling,' she said, and began to scream.

When I heard Mother's weary footsteps on the stairs I turned off the torch and hid my head under the bedcovers. I began to cough violently but managed to smother the noise in my pillow. Mother put Flora back to bed, lay beside her for a while, then went back downstairs. I got out of bed and leant a chair up against the door of my room in case Flora decided to creep about in the middle of the night.

On the top floor of the house there were three rooms: Flora's, mine, and Mother's. The new baby slept in with Mother, in a cot. Once we were all settled down in bed Mother would go downstairs to the sitting room on the first floor and watch telly or listen to her new Beatles LP, quietly, so that if the baby started to cry she would be able to hear her. If Flora or I called down to her she would ignore us. If we persisted she would come out of the sitting room onto the landing and tell us to shut up and go to sleep. Sometimes when I began to cough she would sigh and climb the stairs. If I stopped coughing before she reached my room she would turn round and go back downstairs again. Flora invented a method of getting Mother up the stairs by waking the baby. One night the baby was screaming so loudly I got up to see what was going on and found Flora leaning over the cot, pinching the baby on the upper arm.

Every Monday our class went swimming at Essex Road Baths. I caught a verruca and had to attend the verruca clinic at Popham Street School Treatment Centre. Twice a week after school Mother would leave the other children with a neighbour and take me to have my foot seen to by the nurse. At first I looked forward to these visits – it was lovely to have Mother all to myself, I liked the smiling nurse in her fresh striped uniform, and for the first two weeks the treatment consisted of lying on a high table and having a little dab of acid painted onto my foot inside a ring of pink felt. On the third week the nurse smiled kindly at me and began to chip away at my foot with a scalpel. I began to cough. She waited until I finished coughing then continued. When she had finished she dressed my foot in a bandage and patted me on the head.

'See you next week,' she said, cheerfully.

I had to lean on Mother's arm on the way home because I felt so faint and my foot hurt. I began to dread that nurse with her smiling eyes. At the next visit she got the scalpel out again. The pain was acute. Then during the routine inspection of my other foot she found another verruca. I began to cry. She painted the new verruca with a drop of acid and sent me off with both feet bandaged. I spent that summer on crutches because my feet became infected. Whenever I happen to pass by that area at the back of Essex Road I am glad to see that the council has demolished the Popham Street School Treatment Centre, and no more children will have to suffer as I suffered on that high table under the blade and the smiling eyes of that beautiful nurse.

I didn't like to mention our poverty to my father when he showed up. I asked my mother why she didn't tell him. She said she couldn't. She went out scrubbing floors. Two of the rooms in the house had to be shut up because the ceilings had come down. He sent a man round to photograph us in our house. In the pictures we looked picturesque. At school I was working on a project about the Russian Revolution. I drew a large picture of Lenin and the teacher hung it on the classroom wall.

I ate with shameful relish the contorted slices of baked liver pierced with eyelets of appalling tubes, the green hard-boiled eggs, the pies containing nameless meat that came in two varieties, reddish or yellowish, the flaccid fishfingers, the hot custard, pink custard, brown custard and wobbling mounds of cold custard that the dinner ladies served up on sweating plates, trying to hide my hunger from the other children. I had difficulty choosing a knife from the bucket of cutlery placed on a table by the pudding counter. I searched among the various designs for the one I liked best, a knife with a heavy handle and broad blade, the join clearly defined. I did not like the knives with slim serrated blades almost indistinguishable from their handles, streamlined, lightweight, like small thin people.

My father took me to Harrods to buy a new dress. We left a trail of muddy footprints behind us on the carpet of the children's clothes department. The assistant showed me endless rails of dresses, silks and lace and velvets, each one in its own sheath of polythene, but I refused them. They disgusted me. I left the shop empty-handed. For my birthday I asked for a pair of jeans, black boots and a knife. I went to school with the knife round my waist on a belt. The teacher unarmed me and sent me home. We moved to a new house and I gave up coughing at night.

DAYDREAMING

I did not suffer from teenage spots because the barbiturates I used to take made me so relaxed. The girls at my school cried when Jimi Hendrix died and Mr Burke, who was taking assembly that day, played *Purple Haze* over the Tannoy. Then we all stood up and sang 'Let us now praise famous men and their fathers that begat them.' I was wearing Jesus sandals, flat soles of leather attached to my feet by leather thongs criss-crossing up my legs to the knee. At break I got caught smoking in the cloakroom. I dropped the cigarette and nonchalantly exhaled. The cigarette smouldered on the floor. Raising my sad eyes I smiled bravely at the teacher. I knew that my eyes glistened. I sniffed as if in grief.

'I know how you feel,' she said, putting a hand on my shoulder. The bangles on her wrist gave off the acrid smell of Indian silver and as she bent forward her long hair brushed my face. 'He was such a creative person. And so young . . . I'll leave you alone now. I do know how you feel,' she added, turning to go.

I picked up the cigarette and had another drag. The teacher meant well. I knew that she had let me off because she wanted to be liked. She wanted to be young and wild and free. It made me laugh because I felt nothing.

It was March 1972, a mild clear evening, the exhilarating smell of night air after rain in my face; I was hanging off the 19 bus with both hands on the rail, my hair flying. I jumped off at the junction of Islington Park Street and Upper Street, crossed the road in my green platform boots, walked past the Hope and Anchor, and heard a voice calling my name. A bloke in a maroon velvet jacket was waving at me.

'You're Louis's sister, aren't you?' he said. 'The legendary sexpot schoolgirl sister of that toffee-nosed heap over there? He's had one over the eight, as they say. So to speak. To coin a phrase. In a manner of speaking. Tuinol and Special Brew. Lethal. Have you got a boyfriend? I'm Simon. Call me Si. I would give you a hand getting him home but I've got to see a man about a dog. So to speak. To coin a phrase. In a manner of speaking. Know what I mean?'

My brother was lying on the pavement wearing a pair of silver lamé tights. His hair was long and curled like Charles the Second's and the skin of his face was lead white. A little smile lifted the corners of his mouth and made him look strangely happy. His eyes were half-open. I prodded him with the toe of my boot but his expression remained the same. I knelt down and felt his pulse. He was still alive. I tried to lift him up but he was too heavy for me.

'Stay there,' I said to him, pointlessly. 'I'll get help.'

The smell of frying drifted out of Micky's Fish Bar across the road.

'Hello love,' said Micky. 'Portion of chips?'

'No. It's my brother. I need some help getting him home.'

Micky pulled aside the bamboo curtain hanging across the back of the shop.

'Bert, John,' he shouted.

Bert and John ambled out of the back of the shop and followed me across the road. Bert prodded Louis with the toe of his plimsoll.

'He's alive,' I said.

'That's one thing,' said John.

He bent down, picked Louis up off the ground, and slung him over his shoulder.

''Ere, Bert. You better come an' all. He's a big bastard. Dead weight.'

'Right you are,' said Bert.

We headed off up Islington Park Street.

''Ere, John. Give us a go,' said Bert.

''Ere y'are, then,' said John, transferring Louis from his own shoulder onto Bert's.

'Light as a feather,' said Bert.

'Fuck off,' said John, laughing as Bert staggered under the weight.

'Wanna go?' Bert said, lurching towards me.

'No.'

They looked at one another.

'Charming,' said John.

'Leave it out, she's upset,' said Bert.

When we got home they laid my brother down on the floor in the hall and went away. I offered them a cup of tea because I did not want them to leave but once they had rid themselves of their burden they backed out of the front door and cleared off.

The hall was dark. I wanted to turn on the light but there was no bulb in the socket. My mother was sleeping. She was having an early night. I did not want to worry her so I rolled my brother onto his side so that if he was sick he would not choke on his vomit, stepped over him and went upstairs to bed. I woke at dawn and heard him puking up. The lavatory cistern was gurgling. I got out of bed, crept down the stairs, leant over the bannisters, and saw him below me on the hall floor stretching luxuriously and smiling in the faint light that shone through the pane of glass above the front door.

When I got back from school my mother questioned me.

'Do you think your brother is homosexual?' she asked. 'I found him asleep on the floor wearing a pair of silver tights.'

I put her mind at rest. 'Don't worry, Mum. Its just a phase he's going through.'

'Why was he sleeping on the floor?' she asked me.

'I don't know.' I was lying. To tell the truth would be sneaky. And after all, the last thing that my mother wanted to hear was the truth. So I told her. I was smug. I cast myself as the heroine of the story, the understanding sister, the goody-goody, and so grown-up. When I had finished I ran myself a bath, swallowed a couple of downers and sank into the water. It was lovely, daydreaming in the afternoon, my eyes half-open, waiting for the wipe-out, the soft smudging dullness, so predictable, so measured, so safe.

I hitched down to Brighton on Sunday morning and bought some acid from a man outside the Brighton Belle. The joyful sound of church bells pealing and the salty wind made me feel happy. A woman in a brown trouser suit was walking towards me along the seafront, her face increasing in size and intensity of colour as she approached. Her face was a tomato, one of those meaty Mediterranean ones, scarlet-buttocked and splitting in the ripening sun. I pitched forward and laughed, almost biting into her red flesh with my sharp teeth. The grassy incline, a municipal seaside hillock sloping gently towards the town centre, appeared dangerously steep, so I descended on my hands and knees. I felt like a little sheep, my hair warmed by the weak sun, a blade of young grass in my mouth. I smiled and the grass dropped out of my mouth and stuck, as it fell, to the skin of my forearm. I continued on my journey open-mouthed. Once I had reached the clifftop I lay on my stomach and peered over the edge at the beautiful sea. Far below two men were basking side by side on a broad blue towel. The gulls cried between them and me.

On the way home the van I was riding in got stuck in a jam outside the Sussex General Hospital. I waved to the patients who had climbed up to grin over the wall at the cars slowly passing on the road. The men in the van gave me a cold beer out of a little fridge mounted on a formica plinth behind the front seats. The beer tasted of metal. Surreptitiously I put my fingers in my ears to protect myself from the volume of the music coming out of speakers built into the upholstery and panelling. The men closed the curtains in the van and nodded their heads in time to the beat. No one spoke to me. The music was too loud for speech. I found in my mouth a chewed cud of mashed grass, the colour bled away. In the palm of my hand the pulp of stalks and saliva comforted me. A neat pile of shirts rode beside me on the back seat, lemon-yellow, mauve and pale pink. I put the cud back in my mouth and swallowed it.

When I got home my father was in the kitchen, kneeling down by the fridge, looking for something to eat. My mother was all smiles. I was afraid to speak in case my voice came out all wrong.

'I'll be off,' said my father, a piece of cheese in his hand.

My mother followed him up the stairs to the front door. I heard her sing-song voice calling out to him. 'Goodbye. Goodbye.'

When she returned to the kitchen she sat down at the table with her head in her hands.

'He's eaten all the cheese,' she said, and began to cry.

Double biology, Wednesday afternoon – the lab was brown, I smelt the bilge-like smell of stagnant water, wet metal, brown wood. Algae grew under the lip overhanging the workbench sinks, beautiful green.

I always sat in the same place, by the door, my name gouged into the wood of the bench through white wax polish and peeled varnish, enclosed inside a bulging heart as if someone loved me.

The teacher entered and we all stood up.

'Good afternoon, Mrs Bacon,' we chorused.

'Good afternoon, girls,' she replied. 'Please find a partner to work with and be seated.'

I sat down on my own. I knew that out of the twenty-seven girls in the class one would remain partnerless. I did not want a partner. I wanted to work on my own, to draw attention to myself, to be special.

Mrs Bacon began to give instructions. 'One member of each pair come to the front please.' 'One member of each pair collect a box of instruments from the cabinet please.' 'One locust per pair and no more please.' 'Take turns now, girls.' The instructions amused me. I heard in my head the unsaid words, the words that might have been, that singled me out. 'Rose, you can have a locust all to yourself.'

I lassoed the leg of my locust with a piece of black cotton as instructed and watched the mechanisms of its armoured body as it flew in a little circle round my head. After thirty seconds its leg fell off. The locust managed to propel itself across the lab, leaving me sitting on my high stool with its leg dangling from the end of the thread. The locust landed heavily at the feet of Mrs Bacon, who knelt down beside it and prodded it with her finger.

'It's dead,' said the teacher.

She picked it up daintily between her finger and thumb and dropped it into a glass jar that was standing on her desk.

'I'll pickle it,' she said, lifting a jar of formaldehyde down from a shelf above the aquarium. The chemical smelt rotten. I saw the locust writhe and twitch as it drowned.

In the aquarium two large toads were mating. Mrs Bacon drew our attention to the spectacle in a hushed voice as if our cries might disturb them. We gathered round the tank and watched them solemnly. The male toad was glued to the warty back of the female, his eyes bulging in his head. After several minutes Mrs Bacon stood up and clapped her hands together. 'Now girls, that's enough,' she declared.

We sat at our workbenches and drew pictures of the locust in flight. We copied diagrams of jointed legs out of the textbook and wrote up the experiment. I did not mention the fact that my locust had lost a leg. I untied the thread and stuck the leg into my workbook with a piece of Sellotape.

'Open your textbooks at page one hundred and six,' said Mrs Bacon. 'Dissection,' she read. 'Seven Simple Steps.'

At that moment the door of the lab opened and we all turned round. A big fair-haired girl in a loose dress of brown velvet stood in the doorway, biting her bottom lip.

'Come in, dear,' said Mrs Bacon. 'You must be the new girl.' I stood up and sat down again. The new girl was pale-skinned, pink and golden like a milkmaid. I wanted her to be my friend.

'What is your name?' Mrs Bacon asked.

'Sophie.'

She had a gap between her two front teeth. Her eyelashes were golden. I caught her sleeve as she walked by.

'Come and sit next to me. I haven't got a partner,' I said.

I lowered my eyes to hide the loneliness and longing I suddenly felt.

'One member of each pair come to the front please and collect a specimen,' said Mrs Bacon.

'I'll go,' I said.

I returned to the bench carrying a preserved rat laid out in a plastic container, its wet coat standing on end.

We followed the directions in the textbook, spreading the rat out on the dissecting board, slitting it open from its anus to its chin with the blade of a scalpel, and fastening open the folds of its belly with long pins. Inside the cavity nestled eleven embryos, unborn rats pickled with their mother, blind inside little milky-blue sacs of tissue, joined together by a looping cord.

At four o'clock the bell rang. I linked arms with Sophie and we shuffled along the corridor, dragging our shoulderbags behind us along the floor. The gold crosses in her ears dangled as she tossed back her head and her milky forehead was scattered with tiny freckles. She invited me to go with her to her house, where her mother gave us a plateful of bread and honey, and I listened to her playing the violin.

I could write a whole book about friendship, the story of my best friends over the years in order like the monarchs of history, their reigns ending abruptly or petering out one after the other, next, next, next. My first was a blonde, a tomboy who was in the same class as me at primary school, lithe like a boy, sporty, odourless and clean; I envied her the hygienic purity of her late puberty, her singing voice, her skill at cricket and football, the blonde lights in her hair. Then there were the twins, daughters of a friend of my mother's, a pair of identical nervous girls with blue eyes. The fact that there were two of them and one of me made it impossible for either of them to be my best friend, because they were inseparable – I could not get between them – but they did take me up, rather as married couples take up single people at a loose end, inviting me to spend weekends in the country with them at their grand-parents' house, where we used to wander about in the country-side and write poetry, and to spend the summer at their house in Tuscany, where we swam and sunbathed naked by a secluded pool and they ganged up against me. (I heard them telling their stepmother that I was unfeeling and inconsiderate because, while they had passed a sleepless night during an electrical storm, fearing death, I had slept soundly and roused them cheerfully at dawn out of sleep that for them had only just begun.) The next was a sexually promiscuous thirteen-year-old who made her own clothes, drank gin and tonic, and slept with me in my bed when she stayed the night. Her pubic hair was bristly because she shaved it. Then it was Sophie (that only lasted a couple of months), then much later a girl with ringlets like Medusa, who introduced me to Nietzsche, cropped her hair as I had done and wrote me a nasty letter to terminate our friendship. The next was another blonde, a girl prone to delusions and attacks of hysterical jealousy, who rejected me also.

At the time these painful endings I found folded inside their little white envelopes were a mystery to me; I received them with amazement – the intensity of bad feeling I was capable of arousing baffled me – but now I think I understand how, in the desperation of my search for some kind of perfect trust and closeness, I was doomed to fail because I chose exciting unstable types as objects of my love, by whom I could only be disappointed.

I do meet some of them still, in the street, or at parties given by mutual friends, in pubs, cafés and bars, and I smile politely or brazen it out (I've nothing to be ashamed of, after all) and raise two fingers, jubilant, childish, stupid.

I heard Flora screaming in the middle of the night, my mother's footsteps as she leapt up the stairs, her voice soothing my sister, my brother Louis retreating into his room, and the door closing behind him. I begged my mother to tell me what had happened. Her refusal lent colour to the lurid pictures in my head. I have since asked my sister what went on that night but she can't remember. My mother told me to use my imagination.

My brother Louis was born on April Fools' Day. He developed a taste for caviare and the day after his sixteenth birthday received a case of tins from my father, delivered to the door in the back of a cab. When the doorbell rang it was suppertime; we were sitting round the kitchen table, eating pasta with a sauce of tomatoes and onion. Louis ran upstairs. We could hear the engine of the taxi grumbling outside in the street and the voice of the driver booming at the front door.

'You Louis?' he asked. 'From your father. He said to say Happy Birthday. Happy birthday to you.' The taxi driver was almost singing.

The box was made of grey cardboard stamped with inky blue symbols and decorative Arabic in red felt pen.

'Let's have a look,' I said, leaning on Louis's shoulder.

'Get off,' he said. 'Give me a chance to open it.'

The box contained ten or twelve tins adorned with paintings of silvery fish swimming in blue-grey seas. The plates of pasta lay half-eaten on the table.

'Pass me the tin opener,' Louis demanded.

My mother, who was standing by the french window looking out into the blackness of the back garden, picked the tin opener up off the sideboard and handed it to him.

'Caviare,' said Louis, once the tin was open. He stared at it for a couple of seconds, smelt it, stuck his finger into it, licked his finger and smiled.

'Not bad,' he said. 'Give me a teaspoon.'

We were watching him. He wiped the teaspoon Mother passed him on the tail of his shirt and began to spoon the caviare into his mouth. When the tin was finished he opened another.

'Can I have a taste?' I asked, unable to wait for him to offer, unsure whether he would.

'Hang on, hang on,' he said. 'Give me a chance.'

He filled his mouth over and over again, looking up after every spoonful and smiling until the tin was half-empty. Then he fed us, ceremoniously, a spoonful each, and we were eager as communicants. He ate the last few morsels left in the tin himself, counted the remaining tins, put them in the fridge, and went upstairs. I suppose he wanted to lie on his bed and digest the feast my father had provided. Mother scraped the cold pasta off the plates into the saucepan in which she had cooked it, warmed it up with a drop of water from the kettle and a piece of butter, and dished it up again.

'Do you think you could give me a hand with the washing up?' Mother asked me when the meal was finished.

'No,' I said. 'Why should I? They're your children. It's up to you to look after them. If you don't like washing up you shouldn't have had so many children. Why should I spend my youth washing dishes? It's not my fault.'

My mother got down on her hands and knees and began to scrape a piece of hardened chewing gum off the lino of the kitchen floor. The sound of the Rolling Stones came floating down from my brother's bedroom. Please allow me to introduce myself, I'm a man of wealth and taste.

'Why don't you get Louis to help you?' I asked.

My mother crawled across the kitchen towards the french window as if to get away from me and rested her forehead gently on the floor. I went upstairs to finish my homework.

At about ten o'clock I heard my brother screaming in his room. Mother did not come up the stairs to see what was going on so I assumed that she must have been sleeping. After a minute or two spent listening to the muffled screams I got off my bed where I was lolling on a purple blanket reading *Jackie* and went to see if he was all right. I opened the door of his room and saw him crouching on his bed in the corner, a sleeping-bag pulled over his head. I watched him for a little while then walked over to him and pulled the sleeping-bag off his head. Abruptly he stopped screaming. His face was yellowish, and at first I thought he had poisoned himself by eating too much caviare. What a way to go. I sat down beside him.

'Are you all right?'

He looked dazed, as if he could not remember me.

'I floated out of the window,' he said. 'I was inside the sleeping-bag, the window opened, and I floated out.'

'No you didn't. It was only a dream. A nightmare,' I said.

'A flashback,' said Louis, tears pouring out of his bloodshot eyes.

'Why did you put the sleeping-bag over your head?' I asked.

'To muffle my screams. I didn't want Mother to hear me,' he replied.

I put my arm round his shoulders, picked up a tee-shirt that was lying in a pile on the floor, and offered it to him to use as a handkerchief.

The next night as I lay in my bed, heavy-headed, leaden-limbed, my poor heart stupefied, beating unfelt in my breast as if it belonged to someone else, one of my brother's friends came into my room, and sat down on the side of the bed. His name was Paki Stan, he was a Pakistani, handsome, with long black hair and sharp teeth, incisors devilishly white and pointed, lips liquorice-brown, palms pale, stroking the side of my neck, my shoulder, my breast. I slapped him feebly on the arm but like in a dream I was unable to raise the strength to fight. He sank his teeth into me, leaving blue marks across my chest that reddened to purple, paled to yellow, faded to brown. He bit my lips, shredding the lining of my mouth, and stuck his tongue down my throat until I was retching. The sweat on his brow and upper lip smelt of garlic, his breath and saliva of spices. My sorry struggle didn't put him off. In fact it really seemed to get him going. I reasoned with him, begged and pleaded with him to leave me alone, but he persisted, pushing his fingers into my dry vagina, tweaking my nipples, soaking my ears with spit. His lovemaking left me cold, I did not fancy him, but I could not stop him from climbing into my bed, unzipping his flies and coming into my pubic hair. I could not stop him because I was too weak, too out of it, and besides I wasn't really bothered. What amazes me now is not his audacity, but my own absence.

The first time I met Sue she too tried to snog me, but without much enthusiasm – I think she was just trying to be outrageous, and she gave up when our teeth clashed together. It was at a party given to celebrate the release of one of my mother's friends from Wormwood Scrubs, in a basement off the Caledonian Road. Sue was a good dancer. She was bumping and grinding in the corner with a man who wore his hair like Veronica Lake. My mother sat in an armchair surrounded by children, her own and other people's, sipping punch out of a half-pint glass. My brother Louis was dancing with Sophie, my best friend. He put his arms around her and rested his chin on her shoulder. She was more or less holding him up. When the record stopped she led him to a sofa in a shadowy corner of the room and they began to snog. My mother rose from her chair and took the youngest children home. Once she had gone the man in whose honour the party had been given began to pursue me. I was fourteen, teetering on high heels, my mouth painted purple like a bruise. I danced with him once but as the next record began and he lurched forward to grab me I managed to escape. I wanted to meet a boy, someone thin, kind and gentle, a tall dark one with hazel eyes. I stood in the kitchen with the grown-ups, eating peanuts. Sue came in to use the telephone. Her hair was yellowish blonde, parted in the middle, a wing flicked back over each ear, one red, one green. 'I dyed it with food colouring. Good, eh?' she said, and laughed. 'It's murder at work,' she added. Her protuberant eyes were ringed with kohl, the lids painted in parrot colours under plucked brows. 'Got a fag?' she asked, and took one from the packet I offered. 'I work in the bookies. Mecca. I like it. I like the men you get in there. Losers. Funny, isn't it? I like the losers.' She drew deeply on her cigarette. 'You'd think they'd be sad when they lose, but they aren't. They smile. Or shout at each other. Then they have another go. I like seeing their faces when they watch the race on the telly. They shout at the telly, grown men, as if it'll make any difference. They're sheepish about it afterwards, like putty in my hands. I wind them up, it's the guilt, they haven't got a hope – you can say anything you like to them. They go on and on until they lose everything, then they smile at me, can you believe it, it's not as if it's my fault, sometimes I think they're asking my permission. I let them smile and I smile back at them. They're soft, even the angry ones. They can't fool me because I know how weak they are. I like that feeling. The sympathy, like. I feel like crying, sometimes, it's like a nurse, you have to be detached. They always come back. Over and over again. I like a gambling man – you know where you are.'

'Have you got a boyfriend?' I asked.

'Yes. I'm three months gone. Getting rid of it. He says he's going to join the Foreign Legion.'

'Really? Why?'

'See the world and that. You know, men, the way they carry on.'

There was something about Sue that fascinated me. I found myself drawn to her because although what she was saying was hard to understand she seemed to know so much about men. Mother never spoke to me about men. Also there was something about Sue that reminded me of Mother.

'Look at this,' she said, unbuttoning the front of her shirt. The skin of her chest was blackened and broken, the fresh red weals of cigarette burns dotted about over old scars. She pointed to the fresh burns with a yellow fingernail.

'He loves me, he loves me not, he loves me, he loves me not,' she said. 'He loves me.'

'Did he do that to you?' I asked.

'Sort of. We took turns, over a period of about nine months.'

'Why?'

'I don't know. Why not? I get in the mood every now and again. Really intense. Plus he enjoys it. Sometimes I suck him off while he's having a smoke in bed.'

When Sue had buttoned up her shirt we returned together into the other room. My brother Louis was on his feet again, huddled into a little group with two skinny boys in hipster jeans.

'Hey Louis, I'm going home,' I said. Louis waved at me.

'Where do you live?' Sue asked.

'Up the road. Do you want a coffee?'

'Why not?'

Mother was in the kitchen, her hair tucked between her chin and shoulder to keep it out of her eyes, sewing name-tapes inside a pair of football socks.

'This is Sue,' I said.

They greeted each other and I put the kettle on.

'Where's Louis?' Mother asked. 'He's got his O-level Maths tomorrow.'

'Still at the party. He'll be back soon.'

Mother raised her head from her sewing and listened. There was a row in the street, the thumping bass of a car radio, shouting, urgent footsteps. The front door slammed. Louis almost fell down the stairs into the kitchen and stood panting before Mother, a foam of white spit in the corners of his mouth.

'Lend me a pound, Mum,' he said. 'Get a move on. I've got to go out.'

'I haven't got a pound,' said Mother.

Male voices, stifled, lured me upstairs. The two skinny boys were making themselves at home. One of them, a Keith Richard lookalike, hung about with mystic symbols, was using the telephone, while the other was admiring his back view in the hall mirror, holding my mother's little looking glass in his hand. He was golden-haired and curly, his cheeks unpleasantly chubby, like buttocks.

'Do you mind?' I asked.

The boys ignored me.

'I said do you mind?'

'Bend over, I want to fuck you up the bum,' said the blond boy.

'I'll fuck you up the bum while you fuck her up the bum,' said the other one, putting the phone down.

I laughed. I had a drag on the lighted cigarette he handed me.

'Where are you going?' I asked him.

'Smithfield. The meat market.'

'Why?'

'Do you want to come?'

'No thanks.'

At that moment my brother ran up the stairs. Mother was chasing after him, screaming.

'I'll never forgive you. If you leave now I will never forgive you. Never. Never. Never.' She yelped when she saw me hobnobbing with the boys in the hall.

'And what do you think you are doing, madam?' she screamed. 'You tart.'

'I'm going,' said Louis, following the skinny boys out of the door.

My mother ran into her bedroom, sobbing breathlessly, emitting sighs of anger and pain. I followed her, tried to embrace her, but she could take no comfort from me and sent me away. I went back down to the kitchen. Sue was sitting at the kitchen table, warming her hands on a mug of coffee.

'Sorry about that,' I said.

'Not to worry. We have scenes at home. My dad's a policeman. I'm looking for somewhere to live.' Sue began to stroke her abdomen.

'Hello in there,' she said. She was talking to the foetus, prodding herself in the little lump beneath her waistband, rapping soundlessly on her hard little belly. 'Hello, hello, anyone at home?' Sue bent her head and cupped her hand around her ear. 'I can hear her. She's trying to tell me something,' she said. 'Hello in there,' she repeated. 'Can you hear me? I'm going to get rid of you. Whoosh! They'll suck you out and flush you away.'

'Don't,' I said.

'Oh, Mummy Mummy please don't get rid of me,' said Sue, putting on a high voice, plaintive, wheedling, to represent the voice of the foetus inside her.

'Belt up, Sue,' I said.

Sue smiled at me and continued.

'You've got to go, little girl,' she said, wagging her finger at her distended abdomen. She looked at me and winked, then began to whine out of the corner of her mouth like a ventriloquist.

'Why do you hate me, Mummy? Why don't you love me? I love you, Mummy.'

'Must you, Sue?' I said.

Sue placed her hand on her belly. 'I think I can feel her kicking,' she said. 'In protest.' She grinned. 'Oi, you, pack it in,' she said, cupping her hand over her ear to listen. 'Hark, I think I hear a little voice.'

Sue bared her teeth and grizzled through them.

'Don't kill me. Please don't kill me. Give me life. I want to live. You might grow to love me. How could you do this to me? How could you?' Her voice was shrill.

Sue began to laugh, heartily, throwing her head back, showing the whites of her eyes.

Mother came downstairs, holding onto the bannister like an old woman, and I made her a cup of coffee. She threw the cup at the wall, and stood among the shards of broken china in her bare feet, watching the brown liquid running down towards the floor.

'Leave me alone,' she said.

The next day was Thursday. It was a beautiful spring day, warm and breezy, joyful weather for wandering about in the dusty streets or finding a bit of grass to lie on and look at the sky. I bunked off games (Sophie had bunked off the whole day, missing double physics, probably still in bed with Louis, the curtains closed, leaning on one elbow in his bed, smoking a cigarette, her eyelids heavy, half-closed) and walked along Camden Road, breathing the shimmering fumes, swinging my games kit in a sad bottle-green dorothy bag, across Murray Street to Agar Grove (that reminded me of the flat round dishes of Agar jelly we used in the biology lab to grow cultures), along Market Road (as a small child I had seen cattle stumbling out of trucks parked in the shadow of the clock tower, herded into wooden pens erected in the road and driven across the meadow full of rye grass and buttercups to the abattoir, dropping their steaming dung behind them), across Caledonian Road and round the back of Barnsbury to Chapel Market, where I had arranged to meet Sue in Alpino's for a coffee at three o'clock (it was her half-day).

'This is Dawn, my mate Dawn,' said Sue, as I sat down beside her.

On the other side of the table a broad-faced girl was smiling at me, her red cheeks roughened as if by harsh wind, her fair hair dry and electric, escaping from the jumble of combs and hairgrips holding it back off her face.

'Hello. Sue tells me you've been having a hard time at home. I'm a nurse,' she said, as if to legitimise her concern.

'Oh, it's not so bad,' I said, the creeping heat of welling tears rising to meet her motherly smile, her kindness, the gentle curve of her neck as she leant her head to one side, and her eyes, lying long like almonds, greyish-blue, beneath grave brows.

'Anything I can do to help?'

I could not imagine how she could help me. I turned my head and looked out of the plate-glass window at the passers-by.

'Dawn is very understanding,' said Sue.

I caught my breath, considering for a moment the possibility of forming my feelings into words, of making them real by dredging them up and hanging them out for an airing in the balmy warmth of the spring afternoon, giving them names across the formica-topped table as if they belonged to someone else, but all I could feel was the lump in my throat, a weight on my chest that made breathing a little difficult, and numbness.

'It's all right,' I said. 'It's just a phase I'm going through.'

The two girls looked at each other and laughed.

'I've ordered egg and chips,' said Sue.

'Ooh,' said Dawn. 'I'd love to join you, but I daren't. The weight just sticks to me like glue. It's terrible. We always get chocolates on the ward and I can't resist them. Ernest says he likes me as I am but I'd like to be slim, leggy, sylphlike, like a model. When I see girls with legs up to their armpits and hipbones and everything I can feel my eyes narrowing – I can feel myself going green. It's not that I want to go with other men, it's just that I'd like to be able to have the choice. I'd like all men to want me. I do love Ernest, but it's the age gap. He's so much older, he's a father figure to me. It doesn't really count him wanting me because he would, me being young and everything, if you see what I mean . . . ' She grinned, showing small, even teeth, and raised her reddened hands. Her hands were square-palmed and workworn like my mother's, a few pale freckles scattered across the backs.

'I saw a woman die today,' she said. 'Death makes you put aside all thought of diets and such. She said goodbye before she went. I happened to be walking past her bed at the time so she said goodbye to me. I'd never spoken to her before, I was just walking past her bed on the way to the toilet when she raised her head an inch or two off the pillow and moved her lips. I stopped and bent down a bit to listen to her and she said goodbye and died. She wasn't in the least bit flustered or frightened. Her eyes were open, and her lips, so I closed them and pulled the sheet up over her head. That's what you do when they die. I felt proud, she was so brave, so fearless – she'd had enough by the look of things, but still . . . '

'Have a fag,' said Sue, handing round her packet.

We lit up and sat in a pall of grey smoke, puffing thoughtfully – I was thinking about death.

'What was her body like, once she was dead – was it different?' I asked.

'It was empty,' said Dawn, without hesitation. 'She was gone.'

'Do you mean her soul, or what?' I asked.

'I don't know. Her self, anyway. The human part.'

'Pearls of wisdom,' said Sue.

'Do you like older men in general?' I asked Dawn.

'I suppose I do, really. It makes me feel nice, them being so lucky to have me.' She grinned at me. 'Do you?'

'No. They give me the willies,' I said.

When I had finished my coffee I left Sue and Dawn in the café, their heads together over a bowl of rhubarb pie and custard, making arrangements for Sue's abortion. My new friends. They looked so unalike, Dawn with her gentle face and wise eyes, her piled-up hair, soft floral dress and nurse's shoes tucked under the table, her dimpled elbows, freckled forearms, and hands like my mother's, folded together on the vinyl place-mat; Dawn had a giving look of endless kindness, while beside her Sue's traffic-light hair and parroty eyes did little to mislead me; I could see she was being brave, bearing up, sporting a bold shirt patterned with see-through pink and silver stripes that hardly covered up her scars. I tried to work out what they had in common, my new friends; it was something they shared with my mother, a female mystery, some kind of damage. I did not understand then but vowed on that day not to share with them that nameless burden, the pain they carried so bravely – I did not want to be like them.

The sunny streets of Islington were dreary, familiar – I walked the long way home past the house in Liverpool Road in which I was born (looking up at the dark windows, I remembered the rosy lino on the kitchen floor and the view from my pram, a view obscured by my brother's head), past the house we lived in on our return from abroad, the outside of which was scaffolded and draped with green net, and the one we lived in before we went away (I saw through the curtainless windows a man leaning his elbows on the lid of a grand piano, his nose stuck into a bowl of roses), past the Draper's Arms, Thornhill School, the mica factory, up the steps of our house and through the front door. In my mother's bedroom, off the hall to the right, my little brother and two sisters were watching *Blue Peter*; I could hear Shep the dog barking and the voice of John Noakes, shouting to make himself heard above the howl of the blades of a helicopter. Mum was downstairs, kneeling in a pool of water, a scrubbing brush in her hand.

'Hi, Mum,' I said.

She looked up at me hanging over the bannisters that led

down into the basement and dropped the scrubbing brush into the bucket.

'Hi, Rose,' she said. 'How was your day?'

'Oh, fine thanks. What about you?'

'Oh, you know. The usual.'

'Do you want a hand making the supper or anything? I haven't got much homework. What are we having?'

'I'll do it,' she said. 'It's only pasta. Won't take a minute.'

'I'll wash up,' I said.

She eyed me up and down but said nothing.

'I'm turning over a new leaf,' I said.

'Thank God for that,' said Mother, fishing the scrubbing brush out of the bucket and sighing.

After supper Mother tied an apron round my waist and piled the dishes into the sink. I rolled up my sleeves.

'Get on with it,' she said. 'What a performance.'

'I'm not used to it,' I said, smiling.

'You can say that again,' said Mother. 'Lady Muck.'

When I had finished I went upstairs to the big empty room on the first floor, stood at the window and looked out at the mica factory opposite. I saw a woman poke her head out of a little metal door on the fire escape, take a drag of a cigarette, exhale, and withdraw, flicking the butt into the road where it landed on the roof of a car. I pulled down one of a pair of mattresses propped up against the wall and lay on it. The room was high-ceilinged, as wide as the house, the two long windows opening onto an uneven road, pebbly and potholed, its broken, weeded surface broadening out between the factory and our house to a dead end, flanked on one side by a terrace of ill-matched houses, of which ours was the corner house, and on the other by several two-storey buildings, workshops or garages like big sheds with flats above, and a pair of little cottages, the front doors side by side under a canopy of frosted glass. Climbing columbine on a wall and chickweed grew in abundance at the end of the short road beside a large puddle, its yellow shores of builder's sand littered with bright specks of flaked mica. An old plane tree grew against the wall. Between the grey bricks the mortar was perished almost to dust.

I sighed, lit a cigarette and covered myself with a heap of dusty covers. The windows were open, curtainless; the room filled with the smell of mica, a faint chemical scent, metallic like the smell of the canal at City Road, borne into the room on the evening breeze. I was tired, my eyelids twitching, and so, dressed and unwashed, I settled down to sleep, stubbing out my cigarette on the floorboard beside me, my shoes on my feet.

I woke up because Louis was in the room, with Sue and the two skinny boys. Louis was wiring a pair of speakers into the back of an amplifier, and Sue was rolling a joint. One of the skinny boys gave me a couple of Mandrax and I swallowed them. Louis managed to get the record player working but collapsed into unconsciousness before he was able to choose a record. Sue handed me the joint and put a record on. I can't remember much about what happened. Towards dawn Mother burst furiously through the door, picked up the record player (which Sue had set on automatic so the record, *Beggars' Banquet*, would play over and over again) and threw it across the room. She hauled me by the arm out of the bed on the floor in which I was sleeping naked with Sue and the two skinny boys and sent me upstairs.

From then on I made a habit of sleeping in the big room. I liked to lie down in my clothes by the open window and pass out on one of the mattresses because to sleep like this made a change from the ritual of going to bed I had observed every night from earliest childhood. I wanted to pare down the nightly performance of washing and cleaning my teeth and changing into my nightgown. I dislodged myself from my bedroom on the floor above, a room painted ultramarine, full of the little knick-knacks of adolescence, and enjoyed the discomfort of the big room, my absence of cleanliness, the emptiness, the open windows onto the factory, my face almost touching the floor.

In June of that year I had my first date. I was not wildly keen on the bloke who had asked me out, nor was he mad about me, but I went along out of curiosity, to see what it would be like. Mother kissed me goodbye and wished me luck when the doorbell rang – it seemed she was pleased to see me taking part in the dating game. The boy gave me a box of chocolates to eat in the film – we were going to the pictures. He was wearing a maroon velvet jacket, his name was Simon, and he was interested in me because he thought I came from a rich family. The film we went to see was *Lady Sings the Blues*. I was a big fan of Billie Holliday, but the film left me with a nasty feeling of dissatisfaction. The boy held my hand in the film and afterwards we went out for a drink. I still enjoy the smell of Brut because it reminds me of my first date, but apart from that the occasion was unmemorable. He walked me home and kissed me on the doorstep, automatically, although the kiss was greedy enough, not unpleasant. He said he would call me. We waited a month before we slept together because it took that long for the pill I had begun taking to work. Mother did not express an opinion on him, my first boyfriend, but she made it clear that he irritated her by commenting on the way he smelt so violently of aftershave, his blow-dried hair, the fact that he called his jacket his coat. She advised me to diet, to tone myself down, to make the best of myself while I was young. She said that if she had been beautiful, everything would have been different. I was glad she confided in me but secretly felt she was wrong.

When Sue invited me to her house I felt no less awkward and

unsure of myself; I could hear Sue shouting reassuringly as the chimes of the doorbell sounded, but it was her mother who opened the door, a stout woman in a black quilted housecoat wearing a punctured swimming cap on her head, through the holes of which locks of her hair were hanging.

'Hello, dear,' she said. 'Come in. The kettle's just boiled.'

I followed her into the front room, where Sue's father the policeman was sitting in his vest watching television, a pint glass of lemonade at his elbow.

'Hello, love,' he said. 'Take a seat. Sue'll be down in a minute. She's in the bath.'

I sat down. Sue's mother left the room.

'Tea?' she called from the kitchen. 'How many sugars?'

'None, thank you.'

'Are you slimming? I'm not being funny or anything. Not that you need to. Does she, Arnold?'

'No,' said the policeman, nudging me. 'Unlike some people,' he whispered conspiratorially.

'What was that?' she asked, coming into the room with some mugs of tea on a tray and a plate of cheese-and-pickle sandwiches.

'Never you mind,' said Arnold, and laughed.

Sue's mother put the tray down and handed round the sandwiches. 'Men,' she said.

I was hungry but felt unable to help myself to a sandwich in case Sue's mother made another comment about my weight.

'Go on. Tuck in,' she said, holding the plate in front of me.

'I won't, thanks,' I said.

'Don't be silly, love,' said Arnold. 'Don't be shy. Eat.'

At that moment Sue came in, wrapped in a towel.

'All right?' she said to me. 'Mother, what have you got on your head?'

'I'm going streaky,' said Sue's mother. 'Highlights. Ash blonde.' She put the plate of sandwiches down.

'Nice,' said Sue. 'The stuff stinks. Farty. Eggy. Ugh.'

'Charming,' her mother replied, cuffing her affectionately.

'It's the chemicals in the solution,' said Arnold. 'When the peroxide makes contact with the hydrochlorine it gives off sulphurous gas.'

'Don't go all scientific on us,' said Sue's mother, smiling.

'Come on,' said Sue. 'Let's go up to my room.'

The room was boxlike, painted pink, a pair of brown floral curtains at the window, unlined, half-open, hanging over frilled and sparkling nets. A set of brown furniture lined one wall, made of varnished wood; the knobs of the wardrobe matched the handles of the chest of drawers, moulded out of the same blackened yellow metal. The headboard of the bed was grainy in texture and lightweight, brown like the rest of the furniture, partly obscured by a pair of two-tone cushions, red and black. The candlewick bedspread was brown, to match the curtains. A collection of trolls, gonks and cuddly toys crowded the end of the bed and sat on the windowsill, looking out between the curtains and the glass. The walls were covered with posters and photographs (Keith Richards, Lou Reed). Beside the bed on a small table was a little cactus in an ornamental pot. A framed collage of family photographs was propped against the mirror of the dressing table – Sue with a policeman's cap on her head, Sue's mother in a bikini, Sue as a little girl sitting on her father's knee, her mother to one side looking anxious as if she were just about to smile.

Sue sat down on a padded stool and began to make up her face. I lay on the bed and looked up at the swirls of starburst plaster on the ceiling.

'How you doing with that boyfriend of yours?' she asked, dabbing her face with a small beige sponge.

'I'm not that into it,' I said. 'Nor is he.'

'I've had a bit of the other with him myself, you know.'

'I know. He said.'

'What did he say?'

'He told me.'

'No, I mean what did he say about me?'

'Oh. Let me think. He said you were all right.'

'He said I was all right? In bed?'

'I suppose he meant in bed. We didn't go into details. Are you bothered?'

'No. I couldn't give a toss, really. Just curious.'

'How about Steve? Are you still into him?'

'Totally. We're going to get a flat.'

'Wow.'

'I've got to tell him first, though.'

'Tell him what?' I lifted my heavy head up so I could see her. She was painting a tiny flower on her face with Tippex, four small blobs at the outside corner of her eye.

'Guess.'

'I haven't got a clue.'

'I used to be on the game.'

'Oh. When?'

'Last year, the year before. I gave up when I met Steve in case he found out. I had to move back home. Dawn said she'd tell him unless I stopped because she knew I really liked him. Dawn says I've got to tell him before I move in with him in case someone else does. People know. I've got a big mouth for a start. Boasting about the money and that. Indiscreet. Thank fuck Dawn made me stop.'

'Didn't you want to stop anyway?'

'Not really. I used to like it, funnily enough. Not the actual sex part, that wasn't usually that great, but I liked the money, meeting men with money, the excitement, them wanting me, paying me for it. Can you imagine, they want you so much they pay you. You don't give a fuck about them, it gives you a buzz. It made a change. Most of them just wanted to stick it up me, twenty quid, twenty minutes, all over. I had a few kinky ones, the usual stuff – spanking's very popular, you get extra for that, dressing up, some of the punters don't even want to touch, just look and wank, then the real perverts, piss and shit merchants, I had one who used to get me to shit on a plate, he put salt and pepper on it before he ate it. I didn't fancy that much, or bondage, although its all right as long as it doesn't go too far. I nearly killed one of them once, a fat Arab, I really lost my temper with him. I had one punter who looked just like John Cleese – I did a double-take the first time, but it wasn't him, I used to handcuff him to the bed, hands and feet, and whack him on the bum with a folded brolly. Corny, punters – no imagination, most of them. I put a folded towel under him so as not to mess the bed. It was easy, I didn't even have to undress. I used to get a few knocks and bruises myself sometimes but nothing too strong. That's where the real money is in that game, that and getting fucked up the bum, if you can take it. You have to have a strong stomach and a sense of humour otherwise you go off your trolley.' She laughed.

'Give us a fag, Sue,' I said.

She chucked me a packet of Embassy and a box of matches. Her mother was next door in the bathroom; we could hear the gurgle of the water in the pipes. I lit a cigarette.

'She's rinsing the stuff out of her hair,' said Sue.

Then the noise of the hairdryer reached us from downstairs, and we heard her mother shouting.

'Sue! Sue! Take a look at this!'

The door of Sue's room opened. Her mother stood on the landing, a mass of golden curls on her head. Arnold was beside her, his arm round her waist.

'What a cracker,' he said. 'You've got to hand it to her. My wife.'

Olive, a brown-skinned girl in my class at school, took to relaxing her hair like Diana Ross. She wore lip-gloss, covered her big brown cheeks in powder, shaved her legs and armpits, waxed her bikini line, plucked her eyebrows and the little hairs on her upper lip, wore anti-perspirant deodorant, went without breakfast, ate Limmits for lunch, and spent her lunch-hour doing exercises to firm her bust. Her boyfriend worked in the garage opposite the school, rode a motorbike, and, when the garage wasn't busy, spent much of his time looking at pictures of women, mostly page three girls or clothed models cut out of women's magazines. Olive told me he had become obsessed with one picture, not of a woman's body but of a face, a bleached-out photograph showing little more than two big eyes, unseeing eyes, out of focus, and a blurred mouth, soft lips slightly parted, ready to receive a kiss. In the photograph there was no nose. Olive tried to emulate the woman in the photograph, painting her mouth black, moistening her lips continually with the tip of her tongue, wearing heavy mascara to give herself that big blind vacant look. She worked out that what her boyfriend liked about the woman in the photograph was the lack of detail in her face – there were no indications of what her character was like – he called her a woman of mystery. He said that all you could see in her face was beauty, and that she was lovable. Olive tried to make her own face lovable by emptying it of all expression. She tried to achieve the bleached-out effect by wearing pale foundation. She covered her nose with Hide and Heal as if it were a pimple. She fasted to empty her body, to make herself smaller, and read continually, receiving through the post each month a package of twelve Mills & Boon books, believing that to fill herself with stories would prevent her face from taking on a careworn look; if she numbed herself in this way her boyfriend would not be able to detect traces of feeling in her face. She felt no sadness, no longing, and became like the woman in the photograph, silent, bleached, her lips slightly parted, a woman of mystery.

As for myself, I would have preferred a smaller nose, something a little daintier, more feminine, with tiny round nostrils no one could see up even if they were lying with their head in my lap, the tip gracefully tilted, a few scattered freckles adorning the bridge, but I made do with the one I was born with, nor did it bother me inordinately. A girl in the lower sixth whose nose I had never noticed came to school one day with it done up in a splint and bandages, her eyes bruised and colourful like pansies. It was rumoured that she had had a nose job. The school eagerly awaited the unveiling. Sure enough, after a couple of weeks, the bandages came off and there in the middle of her face was a nose like a little child's, featureless and perfect. She showed it off in the cloakroom and told us it had cost her father nine hundred pounds. I looked at it without envy and viewed its possessor with some disdain because I myself possessed an unformulated and half-conscious belief that nose jobs were not the answer to the general sense of dissatisfaction with which many of us viewed ourselves, a dissatisfaction that in my case had grown as I myself had grown, and that I now associate in my mind with my mother looking at me, head on one side, her eyes narrowed to little hateful slits.

Of course there were girls in the school who had perfect noses without recourse to surgery, particularly in class six alpha, a class containing a higher proportion of school beauties than any other, as if the teachers had streamed them for looks rather than brainpower. These girls, Rebecca Mitchell in particular, and the ones with whom she wafted about, were all slender, with long long hair and soft floppy clothes, drenched in patchouli oil, with dazed eyes outlined in kohl, their velvet skirts and patchwork shawls trailing on the ground. I used to watch them in fascination as they wandered about on the grass by the tennis court, or settled under the mulberry tree, barefoot, sharing a bag of plums or cherries, spitting the stones carelessly into a bush. I envied them their looks, their friendship with one another, the delight with which I imagined they sensed that they were different, special, better, the best.

Another girl who fascinated me was Emmeline King, who wore gold-rimmed round glasses halfway down her nose (the wings of her nostrils were always endearingly reddened), the discs of her lenses a little thicker and much bigger in circumference than those of John Lennon, her school shirts made of special soft cotton, the rounded collars girlish and old-fashioned, the buttons of her cardigan of real bone, her school skirt of bottle-green elephant corduroy, her school bag an old brown leather satchel containing a set of draughtsman's pens in a black zip case and a giant-sized set of professional felt-tips for colouring in her maps and diagrams, a set that contained eleven shades of green alone, twelve if you counted one of the two shades of turquoise. She was in the same class as me for French, and spoke it perfectly, growling the letter R like a native because her mother, a French teacher, was French, and every holiday she went with her family to stay in Corsica, where her father had built a house (he was an architect). I myself suffered from acute awkwardness when speaking French – it was the embarrassment of making those little grunting noises while Emmeline and another bilingual girl in the class chatted away fluently, making French jokes that even the teacher, who was English, was unable to understand. Apart from Emmeline and her bilingual friend it was the posh girls in the class who were good at French. I noticed that the more tastefully dressed the girls were, the more fluently they could converse. Speaking French was glamorous, unlike proficiency in Maths; it divided us up. One afternoon after a particularly painful attempt on my part to describe to the class how I had spent the weekend I saw Emmeline smiling to herself. I thought she was laughing at me but after the lesson had ended she invited me to tea.

When we arrived I was struck by the sheer opulence of the place; the velvety expanses of wall-to-wall carpet, the heavy pelmetted curtains in broad stripes of dark green and brown, the sofas made out of stainless steel tubes and dark green leather, the ethnic rugs and glass jars of orange lilies, the decorative abstract paintings of a kind I knew my mother frowned on, the stacks of glossy hardback books, the stereo with speakers on three-legged stands, the huge farmhouse-style table in the open-plan kitchen on which were arranged in a line down the middle a series of pottery vessels, bluish grey, one holding a dozen lemons, one several enormous artichokes, and the third an abundance of beautiful fruit – polished apples, lychees, downy peaches, apricots and purple plums, piled up and overflowing like the harvest festival baskets we used to fill up at my primary school, each child bringing one fruit or vegetable from home. Emmeline's scented au pair girl invited us to help ourselves. I could tell that we were allowed to eat as much as we wanted, but I restrained myself, out of fear; I did not want my eager greed to show in the face of such plenty, and besides, Emmeline took one peach, nibbled it, lost interest before it was finished, and threw it away.

The smell of scent in general makes me feel sick, but if I catch a whiff of *Femme*, a rich smell, sweet, floral, with a bodily deepness underneath, I feel greedy – the scent excites me with its gorgeous female power, the glamour of the shapely slim-necked bottle folded inside a piece of dark material, buried in Mother's top drawer under her tangled underwear, darkness protecting the volatile fragrance, before Flora and Conrad and Sarah were born, before we went to sea, when we were rich, when there was only Mother and Louis and me. Mother leant over my cot, dreamy-eyed, wearing black lace – I could see through it the pale skin of her chest and the satin straps of her petticoat, there was a trace of cigarette smoke on her breath, from downstairs music reached me, voices and laughter. I had seen the champagne cooling in the bathtub, and the flowers. I tried to encircle my mother's wrist with my hand because I knew she was going out – that was what the *Femme* meant – and as she bent to kiss me I was not sad she would leave me, I was glad because I wanted my mother to be happy, I was happy that men gave her flowers – I wanted to see her laughing.

That sinking feeling – I get it in the morning when the alarm goes off, a drop out of oblivion, down, down, deep pain in the cavity of my chest, my head leans gently sideways, I feel as if the contents of it are left behind, a prickling shower of dust streaming out of my ear like the tail of a meteorite.

That sinking feeling. We'd only been together eight months, Charles and I, eight months of awkward closeness, clumsy, his anklebones digging into my calves in bed, his knees finding the soft muscle of my thigh, his elbow pinning me to the mattress by the hair, and we never talked to each other. I suppose I loved him, but he irritated me – his boyish awkwardness was charming, in a way, but after a while it got up my nose. I used to like the back of his neck, the brown, touching curve of it, the little mole. I kissed the back of his neck and felt him flinch, only very slightly, and then he was too kind all of a sudden, he was talking to me as he had never done before, his voice heavy with concern, solicitous, and I knew. This was it. The words he chose were well thought-out, he was trying to spare me, but as soon as he began I could feel myself sinking, and heard only the meaning behind them – I don't want you. I don't want you any more.

'It's not that I don't still love you, because of course I do. It's just that I feel I need to spend some time on my own, I need to be in my own space, to get my head together. There's a lot of things I need to learn, to understand about myself, a lot of things I need to work out. We can still be friends. I might go abroad – I need to travel – maybe Thailand . . . '

Standing beside him, I don't feel sorrow, nor do I cry. I get that sinking feeling, I feel nothing but heavy downward motion, a dragging descent into nothing, like dying, then like death.

Dusk, a deep blue falling darkness, damp, and the lights were already on in the Princess Royal Nurses' Home. I was outside, before the nightly drawing of the curtains, leaning on cast-iron railings – I've always had a thing about nurses – looking through grey nets, almost transparent, behind which the room was soft and dim, cosy, as if my eyes were full of tears. Small mats were placed here and there on the floor between the brown couches and the big armchairs, making round patches of colour on the dark lino. The walls gleamed, the yellowed gloss paint reflecting light shed from bulbs hanging overhead in yellowed parchment shades. The nurses, mainly out of uniform, sat about in large armchairs, drinking tea, chatting, reading magazines. On the squashed cushion of the window-seat I glimpsed a pair of big knees, the feet drawn up and tucked beneath the stiff hem of a tweed skirt, a misshapen shoe on the floor where it had fallen. I saw a girl rise and smooth the curve of her bottom with a worn hand, tugging the wrinkles out of her skirt. Another, a muscular blonde, narrow-hipped, the front of her blouse gaping, lowered her weary head to rest on the cool surface of a painted table. Before her eyes closed she saw me looking through the window. She didn't smile, although her lips moved. I lit a cigarette, as if to explain my presence on the pavement outside the nurses' home, and went on my way, longing to be in there with them, where you were never alone, where everyone cared about each other.

A home help from the council came in twice a week to help my mother with the cleaning. The woman was fierce, Irish, carrying a tower of red curls piled on her head. She refused to do the heavy work because it was not within the terms of her council employment agreement, but she was prepared to wash dishes, sweep up, and dust. I saw the disgusted angry pleasure in her eyes as she worked, removing dirt, disinfecting, eyes green like mine, pitiless, and the sly glances she gave me, admonishing glances, daggers, asking me why I didn't get up off my fat arse and lend a hand. She would mix up a solution of sugar-soap and hot water in a plastic bucket and scrub the dirty fingerprints off the walls, talking to herself, muttering, the words exhaled on scented breath.

Her hands when she drew off the rubber gloves of her trade were silken and powdered; she smeared them with Nivea when she had finished her afternoon's work, pushed back the cuticles with a pearly-handled instrument, and smoothed the milky skin. The woman was called Mrs Smiley, and she did smile, when it was five o'clock and her day's work was over. She smiled as she held her nicely tended hands to her nose and inhaled, her smeared bluish eyelids lowered in a rapturous reflex as if she were smelling a rose; she smiled narrowly, a smile of secret thoughts, complacent, as she dried her rubber gloves with a little yellow towel she kept in her holdall for the purpose, as she took off her apron, folded it, and put it away. My mother spent every Tuesday and Thursday morning clearing up before Mrs Smiley's arrival so the embarrassment she endured under the scrutiny and judgement of that domestic tyrant would not be too intense. On Thursday afternoons my mother went to see a social worker at the local social work office to discuss her problems. The anti-depressants the doctor had given her made her feel worse so she hid them away at the back of the cupboard on the landing outside my room and Louis and I took them occasionally until they were all gone.

Sue moved into the big room (the flat she was going to share with Steve had fallen through), bringing with her the small brown bed from home, and I moved back upstairs to my bedroom. Steve stayed the night sometimes, uneasily, refusing to use the bathroom in the morning and slipping out before my mother was up. We laughed at his delicacy, the way he tiptoed in deference to my mother's feelings, his adherence to a social code long since dispensed with in our house.

About five weeks after Sue moved in, Steve went off to join the Foreign Legion, promising to stay faithful, promising to write. In his absence Sue developed a glandular imbalance, a thyroid condition with no painful symptoms, making her eyes stick out.

Conrad and the youngest child, my little sister Sarah, who was nearly five, played in the street with the children from next door. There were five of them, like us, five stunted white children who lived in the basement with their parents, the father an asbestosis sufferer, choking in his chair, their mother boiling washing in the back. The children sat on the wall outside their house eating bread and jam and throwing stones into the puddles in the road. Their mother seldom emerged from the shed, a corrugated iron and breeze-block back extension fitted out with a Burco wash-boiler and a Baby Belling running off power drawn from an extension cable looped across the ceiling on a series of cuphooks. She cooked and washed all day long and much of the night, making lumpy soups out of bones and pearl barley, and boiling up her husband's handkerchiefs. I saw her a few times out of my bedroom window in the yard, wrapped in a dark red dressing gown, a pair of men's shoes on her feet, her mouth full of wooden clothespegs, hanging winceyette sheets on the line, but I had never seen her out in the street. Elaine was the oldest daughter, a couple of years younger than me, a thin, witty child who enjoyed the self-possession her mother lacked; she used her natural talents to make up to her brothers and sisters for any loss caused by the refusal on the part of her parents to face the world outside their damp little flat, and seemed only amused by their deficient wits. She was quite willing to relieve her mother of the responsibility of negotiating the whys and wherefores (as she called them) of the outside world, and looked on her lot, as the organiser and provider of her family, as a position with perks; the hard work and difficulties she was forced to take on brought with them a reward – power and money, a door opening into the adult world. After school Elaine wheeled their old pram through the streets to Chapel Market for potatoes and onions, mince or streaky bacon, collected the National Assistance from the post office, and fetched her father's racing paper from Madge's on the corner of Hemingford Road where I used to do my paper round.

Saturday afternoon, Elaine was hanging about outside the off-licence in her red cardigan, a handful of coins in her outstretched palm; she was trying to catch the attention of the people going in and out of the shop, hoping someone would be kind enough to get a few bits for her – she had to get a packet of Player's Weights for her father, a miniature of whisky, and four bottles of barley wine. She held out the money to show she wasn't begging; she couldn't go into the shop herself because she looked too young to get served. A woman took her money and came out with the brown bag of bottles. Elaine opened the packet of cigarettes on the steps, sat down under the awning on the reef of pebbled concrete marking off the shopfront from the pavement, lit up and inhaled deeply, enjoying a moment of peace and quiet, the fresh damp air of the evening, the longed-for comfort of the cigarette. When she looked up and saw me crossing the road she held up the cigarette between two fingers like a beacon, beckoning me. I joined her on the step and took the proffered butt. We walked home together.

'It's face the music time for me,' she said, descending the steps to the open door behind which her father was waiting. I heard her telling him she had opened the packet to give one to the lady next door, because the poor soul was gasping. The poor soul was my mother. Her father tried to whack her across the back of the legs with his rolled newspaper for lying but she had no difficulty avoiding his feeble blows. I heard curses and his wet cough as I climbed down the steps to our side door. Elaine came bounding out from behind the straggling privet hedge that grew out of a heap of pressed grey mud in front of their house and winked at me.

The side door of our house was unlocked, the flaking paint dull green, like poison. I opened it and heard my mother call out from the kitchen.

'Hello. Who's that?'

'Me.' I heard her sigh in the silence, a long weary sigh as if I were the last person on earth she wanted to see.

'Hello,' I said.

'Oh, hello,' she replied, with effort, as I entered the kitchen. My mother was chopping onions, a narrow-bladed knife in her hand. She looked up slowly from the white heap of slices on the board and showed me her blue-grey eyes. Her eyes were full of tears. I gazed into them and I was frightened. It frightened me to see her crying, mouthing soundless words at me, her mouth a little twisted. I was unsure of myself, but I knew that if I looked away she would begin to scream. I knew she would be the first to lower her eyes and I was right – I outstared her and she returned to her chopping, the blade moving swiftly against the nail of her index finger.

'I'll put the kettle on,' I said.

I filled the kettle and struck a match to light the gas. I couldn't think of anything to say. I wanted to cheer her up or bludgeon her over the head with an iron bar. While I was turning away from her towards the stove I could feel her eyes on my back, appraising me, taking in the waistless back view I presented miserably to the world, the big round buttocks, and my short neck – a view I had never seen myself but one she had described to me often enough.

'Do you want a cup of coffee?' I asked.

'No.'

I made myself a cup of tea and sat down at the table to drink it. My mother's tears were falling faster now, splashing onto her hands. Abruptly she stopped chopping, and began to play with the knife. I watched her pass it from one hand to the other, over and over again, like a murderer in a film. I thought she was trying to frighten me, toying with the sharpened knife, and she succeeded. I wanted to run away from her, from the pain she was suffering, her misery, our poverty, and the fear. I sipped my tea, my legs shaking under the table.

'What's the matter?' I asked.

She did not answer me.

'Why are you crying?'

'It's the onions,' said Mother.

She rose from her chair, hesitated for a moment, dropped the knife on the floor, laughed, cuffed me gently on the back of the head as she passed and ran up the stairs, wailing.

Things began to disappear from my room, only little things, but I missed them; a plum lipstick, the matching eyeshadow, a glass vial of tuberose oil, a tortoiseshell hair comb, a black velvet ribbon, a picture postcard of Marlon Brando, a powder puff, the empty box in which some soap had been given to me (the cardboard impregnated with the smell of carnations), and a paperback copy of *Emma* by Jane Austen. At first I thought the disappearances were the result of absentmindedness on my part, a series of careless accidents that were a side-effect of the dazed state in which I passed my time, each inexplicable loss adding to my sense of confusion, but after several total room searches and experiments which involved leaving something tempting in an obvious but not too obvious place in my room, memorising its existence and position by staring at it for several minutes, then going out for the evening, I realised that someone was stealing my things. This discovery pleased me; I no longer had to hold myself responsible for the losses. It was a relief to find I was not the source of the disturbance, like a poltergeist, fragmenting the bits and pieces of my world. And I knew who the thief was – the only other person in the house who would want my girlish bits and pieces, my small poor collection of things, each one loaded with significance for me. It was Flora. I recognised her covetousness – she wanted my loss as well as her own gain – and saw she was caught up like I was by longing to possess, a secret greed, ravenous, shameful, bottomless. I went into her room when she was asleep and while her noisy exhalations reassured me I searched her chest of drawers. There I found all my things, unused, hidden together in the back of the bottom drawer. The theft made me angry but I did not wake her. I took my things back to my room, spread them out on the table, moved them from one position to another, and turned them over and over and over. I had the same feeling when I put some money on the dogs last year and won; Louis gave me a tip, I came out of the bookies with one hundred and seventy-six quid in my pocket, elation, I paid the phone bill, bought a pair of shoes, and yet it didn't really make any difference to me, I felt a bit sad.

Yesterday evening while I was ironing a shirt in the kitchen of my new flat I became aware of a woman's voice on the radio, a hollow voice, echoing clearly out of the muddle of sound-effects and music to which I was more or less oblivious, separating itself from all the other voices by a quality of delivery so piercingly pitched I paused to listen.

'This innocence is sort of Christian,' said the woman, taking a breath, audibly, before continuing. 'You know, in the Bible the poor are holy. The broken can't be spiteful. No one could be jealous of me, I protect myself from attack by surrounding myself with children, who can blame me – I have so many mouths to feed it makes me feel like Jesus. No one can blame me – I can't even remember what it is like to make choices. Desire died on me, ages ago, I got out of practice. Now I am desireless and numb. It is not my fault, nothing is my fault. I am a mother. You can't expect me to be able to stop crying. How can I be responsible for my own actions when I am so lonely, so poor, so broken? No one can hold me responsible for anything because I am doing my best. Anyway, I am really a very strong person, underneath it all. How else could I bring up all these children on my own? How else could I have taken so much pain? How else could I have gone on suffering? I scrub floors with my own tears. You are cruel and heartless to expect me to be able to stop crying, after all I am dressed in rags, I dress myself in rags because I hate myself and I have a right to cry. When I am undressed I hate myself even more. The sight of myself naked makes me feel depressed. Even when my body was young and unmarked by childbirth I hated it. When I have a bath I keep my eyes closed to shield myself from myself. I have few friends because I hate most other people as I hate myself. People whom I suspect might be worthy of admiration make me feel so unsure of myself, so jealous, so ugly. I narrow my eyes and scrutinise them, looking for faults. I know, I know it's not very nice. I feel safe with the working classes, because they do not judge me. Black people also are easier to deal with. People who are broken down I find attractive, they make me feel stronger, but they are by nature unreliable, and in the end their weakness makes me resent them – I despise their bad habits, I want to change them, they irritate me, and with the last vestige of strength remaining behind after my self-respect has left me I send them away, or they leave me for someone else. I eat only bread, half a loaf at a time, and the little pieces of rind, the burnt bits, gristle and crust the children leave on the sides of their plates, because I like to bloat my stomach with food that does not nourish me properly or go hungry because that is what I deserve. I know I have a sharp tongue, I admit it, but it is not really my fault – I am not a spiteful person; sometimes it is as if this piece of red flesh in my mouth was disconnected from the rest of me, like a mouthful of meat I have bitten off and am unable to swallow.'

When I heard the woman say that she scrubbed floors with her own tears I began to suspect she was playing a part because of the miserable theatricality of her choice of words, the way she delivered her sentences as if they had been rehearsed, but I realised that her high-pitched voice was hollow and distant because she was talking on the telephone – I was listening to a phone-in on LBC. The woman finished speaking and there was silence on the air, a shocked silence broken after about ten seconds by the sound of Brian Hayes clearing his throat and saying, 'Well, I don't really know what to say.'

When my grandmother (on my mother's side) was depressed she took to her bed and I too have developed this habit. I might lie down for a little rest, half-dressed, a cup of tea beside the bed, to read, or close my eyes if I am tired and find myself sleeping, waking and sleeping until I am hungry. Then I rise, bathe, eat and close my eyes again in the bed in which I find myself. I daydream.

I was dancing with a boy at a party, a slow dance, it was hot in the room, St Patrick's Day, Paddington, 1978. I closed my eyes and smelt his biscuity smell like Rich Tea. Behind my back he held a lighted cigarette, the ash growing longer and longer, my chin resting on his shoulder, his hair curling on his collar. His name was Pat, Patrick Mangen, a painter and decorator who used the café where I worked in the Edgware Road. He was wearing a red shirt and casual trousers, belted, the bottom half of a suit, and a little chain around his neck with a crucifix on it. His hair was wavy, his eyes calflike and mild like a saint. After the dance he held my hand and led me over to the table under the window where we had left our drinks.

'Egg bacon sausage chips and two slices,' he said, laughing. That was the breakfast he ordered every morning. Every morning I buttered his bread for him, cut it in half diagonally, and slid it onto a small plate. I knew he liked his egg a bit crisp on the bottom. I knew he had three sugars in his tea. When Giovanni the chef called out the cooked order from the back kitchen and banged the plate down on the shelf of the hatch I enjoyed coming out from behind the high counter, my long white apron tied tightly round my middle, a plate in each hand, to serve Patrick Mangen, the Blakies on the heels of my boots tapping on the floor. Sometimes when I served him he didn't even look up from his newspaper to thank me. Sometimes he let the food go cold in front of him while he finished a cigarette. He hadn't noticed me. I couldn't make him notice me. I thought perhaps he had mistaken me for a boy, because of my cropped hair, my jeans, my boots. The insides of his arms were pale, bluish, emitting soft light. Now I held one of his big hard hands in mine. He was smiling at me. He had bad teeth; one of his front incisors was brownish, broken and rotting, unlike my own great shining tombstones, a sign of his otherness; looking back, I found this attractive, manly, like his tattoos.

'Do you like me?' he asked, turning to face me, catching up my free hand in his.

'I do,' I said, lowering my eyes.

'Look at me,' he said.

I looked at him. He was drunk, his breath smelt sweet and beery, his eyes were bloodshot. He was wearing a little piece of twisted wire in the hole in his left earlobe. He leant forward, pressing against me, his chest heavy on mine.

'What's your name?'

'Rose.'

'Rosie, Oh Rosie,' he sang, his lips almost touching my ear. 'Do you know you're a beautiful girl? Round the eyes, in particular. Did anybody ever tell you that before?' He picked up his can and poured beer down his throat, swallowing again and again until it was all gone. Then he put his arms round me and kissed me on the lips, tentatively, withdrawing quickly, as if he thought I might slap him. He looked at me for a moment to gauge my reaction then kissed me again, this time letting his dry lips move against mine. I stroked his back gently with one hand and slipped the other one round the back of his neck, beneath his hair, where the skin was damp. He pushed the wet tip of his tongue between my lips and licked the inside of my mouth. His hands were moving up and down my sides, touching the underside of my breasts, smoothing the top of my thighs. I began to swoon against him, and my knees trembled. He pulled his mouth away from mine and sucked in a long deep breath.

'Do you still like me?' he asked, unsure of himself in spite of the drink in him.

'Yes,' I said.

'Do you want another drink?' he asked, pulling the top off a can of beer, and holding it out to me. I took it and he opened another one for himself. Then he put two cigarettes in his mouth, lit them, and handed one to me. Together we leant on the windowsill and looked out at the estate below us, the patches of thin grass bordered by small green fences, the concrete paths, the dull brick blocks of flats in darkness apart from the blue glow of municipal lighting in the entrances and staircases, the roofs of cars parked on white marked lots.

'Well, it's a beautiful world we live in,' said Pat. 'Look at the sky.'

He pointed upwards, above the roofs and telegraph poles, between a pair of tower-blocks in the distance. The sky was heavy yellow-black, a uniform colour of unbroken dirty cloud, and moonless.

'A thing of beauty in itself,' said Pat. 'Like you.'

We had another dance. It was the same record as the time before, I'm in love and I love the feeling. Patrick Mangen was singing it to me in my ear as we danced. He was holding on to me so tightly I could feel my ribs bruising. Each time he stumbled we nearly fell over. Some of his friends were leaning against the wall, whistling and cheering. When the record was finished I left him in the middle of the floor, his feet slightly apart as if to steady himself, and went to find the lavatory. The hall was dark, the air thick with the smell of air-freshener and old carpet. A girl who worked with me in the café was leaning against the wall, sipping a brown drink from a chunky glass.

'Linda, where's the toilet?' I asked.

'Second door up the passage.'

'Having a good time?'

'You are, I can see that,' she said. 'Glad you came?'

'I am. Thanks for inviting me.'

'Seems to like you, that bloke. The one from the café.'

'I know,' I said.

'You look nice,' said Linda. 'Sort of happier than usual.'

'You look nice too.'

'Thanks. You go next,' she said, as a couple came out of the lavatory, the man zipping up his flies.

The cubicle was small, painted avocado green, the back of the door decorated with pictures of dogs and cats cut out of magazines. Above the cistern on the narrow windowledge there was a bottle of Harpic, a rusty aerosol of lavender furniture polish, and a cellophane packet containing three bars of carbolic soap. Across the window on a short length of mauve ribbon stretched between two cuphooks a piece of net curtain was hanging, behind which a dead fly was trapped against the glass. I sat on the lavatory, my head in my hands, and spoke to myself as if there were two of me, because I was drunk.

'This is me,' I said. 'Me. Hello, me. Hello.'

The sparkling blackness, pressed against my eyelids by the palms of my hands, began to spin and make me feel sick. I raised my head and opened my eyes, blinked, and looked at my big pale thighs spreading on the plastic seat, and the small patch of curly hair at the neat point where they met, as if the weighty flesh and female softness did not belong to me. I found the sight repellent, almost erotic.

'Hello. Hello, Rose.' I spoke to myself as if I were someone else. I don't ever get that feeling any more. When I had finished pissing I pulled up my knickers, zipped up my trousers, and pulled the chain. There wasn't any paper. I could feel a small wet patch spreading in my knickers. Outside in the corridor Linda was snogging with a red-haired boy. The front room was dark, lit only by a red-shaded lamp glowing under the table. Patrick Mangen was leaning out of the window, looking out at the yellow night, smoking another cigarette. I went and stood beside him. He turned to face me and in my mouth I caught some of his tobacco breath as he exhaled. He looked distorted in the half-light before dawn, his face pale and hideously ugly, one eye lower than the other, his nostrils unpleasantly open, the thin broken teeth shining in his red mouth. But when he smiled at me, a wide warm smile of complicity, I smiled back because I wanted him, ugly or not; I wanted to spend the night with him, the night he thought was beautiful.

On the way home he produced out of his back pocket a set of miniatures in a tartan presentation case, eight little bottles of spirits that when opened gave off a potent vapour of alcohol warmed by the heat of his body. I had a sip or two of whisky, just wetting my tongue, while he poured the bottles one after the other down his throat. I thought he might die on me but the alcohol seemed to enliven him. He flung his left arm around my shoulders, almost knocking me down, and blew kisses at the windows of the upper storey of a tower-block. I encircled his waist with my right arm, and together we stumbled along the broad pavements of the Edgware Road, blown about like litter by the wind. Night workers returning from their shifts and early-morning cleaners, carrying their equipment and overalls in little holdalls, stepped into the road to give us room to pass. We meandered along by the side of the canal and staggered down sidestreets, falling once or twice. As we turned the corner of my street and I began to fish in my pockets for the key of my flat, Patrick looked at me a little sadly.

'How you feeling?' I asked him.

'On top of the world.'

Once the front door was open we crept along the hall, past the door of the ground-floor flat, steadying ourselves against the wall. Patrick knocked over the spindly hall table, scattering a Grecian-style dish of plastic roses onto the dusty carpet.

'I beg your pardon,' he said, formally, as if to belie the fact that we would soon be together, naked, strangers, in my double bed. I overtook him at the bottom of the stairs and he followed me up to the top of the house. I turned the light on in my bedroom and sat on the edge of my bed, taking off my boots. He came and sat beside me, motionless, staring at the wall.

'How you feeling?' I asked him.

'Don't keep on asking me that,' he replied, slowly untying his shoelaces.

'I'm just going downstairs to the loo,' I said.

In the bathroom I cleaned my teeth, drank out of the tap and splashed my white face with cold water. A lemon-scented geranium growing in a pot on the side of the bath filled my head with its fragrance. I bruised one of the hairy leaves between my fingers and breathed in the smell. I felt desire, disbelief, hunger aroused by the smell of the plant, and climbed the stairs. The air in my room was rich and strange. Patrick Mangen lay in the bed, open-mouthed, his eyes closed. I took off my clothes and slipped in beside him. He was unconscious, breathing gently; I lifted the covers and saw that he was wearing a pair of dark brown underpants. I felt warm towards him, almost loving; he was sleeping so peacefully. I stroked his forehead and remembered, with a smile and a sharp exhalation of breath, almost a snort, as I fell asleep, how hard it had been, earlier on in the evening, to imagine him in my bed with me, putting his hand between my legs, kissing my nipples, pushing his erect penis inside me.

Warm reddened sunshine seeped through the crimson fabric of the curtains, through my closed eyelids between sleeping and waking, and my limbs were curled, comfortable, lifeless beneath the weight of thick covers. I swooned – a warmth as of hot liquid washed over me, emanating from the man beside me, like blood bathing me, or milk, gentle, floating me amniotically, body heat, so nourishing, a mystery. When I woke up, at noon, parched and aching, I found myself lying in a wet patch. Pat, fully dressed, was sitting on the edge of the bed with his back to me, fumbling with his shoelaces. I let him go, pretending, as he tiptoed across my room to the door, that I was still asleep; I wanted to spare him – he had pissed in my bed, and I never saw him again.

I was walking behind a black woman in a grey zip-up car-coat. She was tallish, of average build, and looked like an American tourist because of the mannish felt hat she was wearing and the small flightbag slung aross her shoulder. Her hair was brushed flat under the dented crown of the hat, although at the back of her neck above the collar of her jacket a few of the oiled and flattened strands were beginning to puff out. She was wearing corduroy trousers and chainstore trainers made out of dark-coloured materials, like her jacket, designed not to show the dirt. The woman was walking very slowly, idling in the sunshine, so I too slowed down. There was something provocative in her walk; she was trying to draw attention to herself by displaying so openly her lack of purpose; and by moving along in the middle of the pavement at such a leisurely pace she was making it impossible for me to pass no less effectively than if she were barring my way with both arms outstretched. In front of us a large man in a vest was crossing the pavement towards the front door of a block of flats. His bulk was soft, unmuscled, the folded fat of his chest like tits, his gut distended as if pregnant. Between his lips the butt-end of a roll-up was hanging, the dead ashes white. The woman turned her head slightly and wolf-whistled at the man. He carried on walking as if he hadn't noticed the incongruous sound issuing from her pouting mouth. For me the woman had unalterably separated herself by her ironic gesture from the usual herd of tourists blocking the streets around the British Museum. I drew abreast of her as the pavement widened and turned to see that she had covered the dark brown skin of her face with heavy pan-stick, a masklike coating of greasepaint the colour of top of the milk. Her eyelids were smeared with layers of pale blue eyeshadow and her cheekbones decorated with two elongated circles of violent rouge. I wondered what induced her to adorn her face so recklessly. The smug way she smiled showed she thought she looked beautiful. Since then I have seen her many times, always painted like a Barbie doll, wandering the streets, smiling with pleasure at her own appearance, with nowhere to go.

Outside the swimming baths in Shaftesbury Avenue, moving towards the benches at the top of Neal Street where the homeless and the alcoholics congregate to drink and enjoy the summer sunshine, I found myself following a couple of bottle-blondes, a man and a woman whose intimacy was displayed in the shared buttery shade of their peroxide hair. The woman's hair was long, the stripped and airy tresses falling in a great mass of shining yellow almost to her waist. The hair of the man beside her had the same yellow dryness, identical, growing strong and lively from his big head like a plant. He was wearing a fancy jersey decorated with rows and rows of beige knitted sheep on a background of chocolate-brown and a pair of low-slung jeans revealing the cleavage of his buttocks. The woman wore gold rings on her fingers, and was dressed like her boyfriend in jersey and jeans. Their clothes and skin were unwashed, they were sharing a can of Tennant's Super, they were holding hands. I imagined them together over a basin in the men's hostel, sharing the sulphur-ous contents of the twin bottles in a home hairdressing kit, the bleach and the activator, taking turns to massage each other's heads, not bothering with rubber gloves. Greeting friends, they passed the benches at the top of Neal Street and crossed over the road towards Apollo Stores. On the zebra crossing they waved like royalty and mouthed thanks to the driver of the waiting car. They stopped suddenly outside the super-market and I was forced to continue on my way. As I passed them I saw their faces. The man was in his twenties, his broad face blurred yet handsome, his eyes half-closed as if he could not take the sunshine. The woman, her ringed hand on his forearm, was almost sixty by the look of her, old enough to be his grandmother, her blue eyes watery, full of love. Their yellow hair marked them out from the other tramps and dossers, the nutters, the homeless and the alcoholics; they had given themselves a bit of crazy glamour, the woman's waist was tightly belted, they walked side by side into the supermarket with their heads held high like angels, making a little sensation at the cash-desk, flaunting their intimacy, drinking Tennant's as if it were nectar. A week or so later I saw them again, sleeping at midday on a bench, his head in her lap, her head in his.

Later on that day I saw a woman lying on her side on the pavement of New Oxford Street, her head resting in the palm of her hand, her pack beside her on a wooden bench, looking at the small photographs from the Paris catwalks in a copy of *Harper's & Queen*, her lips parted with hunger to absorb the new shapes and colours of the season. The lower part of the woman's face was mostly painted scarlet; a smeared smiling lipstick mouth, applied with little regard for the contours of her own lips, stretched clownishly from ear to ear. She was wearing a jersey on her head as if it were the headgear of some elaborate national costume, giving her a faintly religious air like a nun or a Rastafarian; the ribbing of the neckhole framed her face, the waistband was tucked in at the nape of her neck to enclose her hair, the stripy sleeves hung down on either side of her head. As I approached she rose langorously from the pavement, swept up the thin patchwork cloth on which she had been lying, and wrapped it around her shoulders with a gesture of weariness and genteel disdain. Then she sat down beside her pack, placed the magazine on her chest, folded her arms across it, and closed her eyes. I lingered by the bench because I wanted to have a good look at her. The woman's skirt was patchwork like the cloth in which she was wrapped, an extraordinary garment made of scraps of threadbare filthy

shirting, bald colourless corduroy, and crisp new strips of
Madras cotton, orange and blue. The squares and rectangles of
assorted fabric were laid out edge to edge, rows of neat black
stitching marking out the perimeter of each patch, hand-sewn,
or unhemmed and overlapping like the fluttering feathers of a
dull bird. It was clear from the various ages of these materials
and the uneven amount of pavement dirt rubbed into them that
the skirt was not a completed garment, finished and uniformly
decaying, but a treelike thing, shedding and renewed with the
seasons, its shape and colours changing like the Paris fashions.
The woman's painted smile was reminiscent of the perfect lips
of the woman on the cover of the magazine, smiling lips,
emblematic, sexual, a disguise.

In front of the homeless men's hostel on the corner of Endell
Street and Shaftesbury Avenue I saw a young woman lying
face-down on the pavement, unconscious, under an open
window, as if she had slipped and fallen while trying to climb
in. At first I thought the woman was a boy because she was
buttockless, narrow-hipped, her thighs concave in her jeans,
but then one of the homeless men who was staggering past
towards the off-licence stopped and turned her over and I saw
her bloated gut swelling over the top of her waistband,
unmistakably female, a mass of yellow spongy flesh. The man
knelt beside her on the pavement and twisted her ear between
his fingers until it was white but the woman didn't flinch – she
felt nothing. He pressed his head to her chest, shrugged his
shoulders, stroked her on her back. His hand was nicotine-
brown to the wrist, kippered, the middle finger ringed with a
band of stainless steel in which was set a slither of greenish
stone or opaque glass. Gently he stroked the hair at the nape of
her neck and uncovered a tattoo, the outline of a broad-bladed
sword, and some words, the blue writing of ink rubbed into
little wounds. With his ringed finger he traced the words of the

motto as if he had difficulty reading – Tomorrow You Will Die. He looked up at me from his squatting position on the pavement and pulled a face, clownlike, an expression of exaggerated misery. I smiled. He stood up, opened his hands palm-upwards to the sky, and wandered off. I phoned an ambulance from the newsagent on the corner and waited outside the hostel for it to turn up, leaning against the wall by the open window, keeping an eye open for the ambulance, keeping an eye on the woman. The flesh of the woman's hands was bluish and blotched red, the backs swollen and mottled, marked with scars and little bruises, the knucklebones misshapen, crushed. Out of the elasticated cuffs of her brown leather jacket her wrists protruded, one circled with the congealed blood of a fresh graze, inflicted with a piece of glass, and the other marked with the white lumps of old scar tissue. A passer-by, a young boy in a brown suit, stopped and asked me if she was dead. I shook my head and he went on his way. I wondered whether I should pick her up, whether I could bear to take that filthy junkie body in my arms and walk her round as I had heard you were supposed to do, but I decided against it; she might have broken bones, I might really hurt her, she might wake up and attack me. I stood near her, at a small distance, watching the pedestrians walk round her body or step over it. Some did not see her. I hoped she would not die because of my decision not to move her, a decision made partly out of squeamishness, my cowardice. By her head was a black bin-liner, burst as if someone had thrown it out of the window, spilling its contents onto the pavement – a soiled blanket, some orange curtain fabric, a blue open-knit cardigan with toggle buttons, and a pair of men's shoes. A man in a tartan sports jacket stopped, rummaged in the bag, picked up the shoes, measured them against the soles of the plimsolls he was wearing, and carried them away. At first I thought that he was stealing the belongings of the woman on the pavement, but then I saw that the shoes would have been of no use to her – they were much too big. I had associated the bag of bits and pieces with her because of its proximity, and because it looked as if she might have thrown it out of the window of the hostel and jumped after it, but now I was unsure. I could not imagine her wearing that ugly blue cardigan with its white toggles and baggy pockets showing balls of crumpled tissue through the open weave – in spite of her dereliction she had retained a certain hard style. The hair on her head was vigorous, a tufty bush two shades of orange-brown, and when the ambulance men came and moved her I saw that her lower back was covered in tattoos, not blue DIY ones like the one on the back of her neck but proper ones from a tattoo parlour, multi-coloured, traditional subjects, a mermaid and a ship in full sail, hearts and flowers, Mum and Dad. The ambulance man who held her in his arms and tried to coax her back to consciousness was tattooed also, on both forearms. The driver of the ambulance drew on a pair of rubber gloves, examined the woman's wrists and forearms, straightened her little legs, felt her scalp for wounds. He spoke to her kindly, calling her darling. Between them the two men lifted her up and leant her against the wall. She seemed to be taking some of her weight on her legs, although her head was still hanging. The man with the tattoos caught up a handful of her hair and raised it so he could look at her face. Her face was pasty, unsexed, the eyes closed.

After a while she managed to speak.

'Daddy,' she said. She spoke in a Glasgow accent. 'Got a spare twenty pence?'

I said goodbye to the ambulance men and left her in their hands. I knew they would look after her. As I crossed the road I felt a choking sadness, and shed tears. Something about that woman drew me to her, although she disgusted me. And she was the one going off in the ambulance with those kind men, to be looked after, as I wanted to be, not me.

Friday night, I am looking out of the window, the pubs are closing and there is a fight in the street outside my flats. A man is hitting a woman about the head with an empty bottle. The woman is backed up against railings, raising her hands to protect herself. The bottle breaks, the skin of the woman's face breaks and begins to bleed. The backs of her hands are slashed, she falls to her knees, keels over, lies on the pavement. The man begins to kick her along the street, he is shouting, she rolls over and over. I run down the stairs of my block, eight flights, but by the time I reach the bottom the man has gone and the woman is being interviewed by the police. Lying on the floor with a policeman kneeling beside her, bleeding heavily, she refuses to identify the man. From the doorway I can hear her repeating herself again and again. 'My man. My man. My man.'

When the ambulance arrives she is reluctant to get into it. The policeman and the ambulance driver lift her onto a canvas stretcher and fasten webbing straps across her chest and legs, so she is unable to struggle or hurt herself.

A tinker woman stopped my mother in the street and my mother gave her money.

'Thank you, bless you,' said the tinker. 'I can see you are a good woman. I can see you yourself have fallen on hard times.'

My mother laughed but I could see in her face she was surprised. She was surprised to discover that just as she found herself drawn to the outcasts and have-nots, the hungry, the needy, the lonely, they recognised her as one of their kind. I wanted to embrace her there on the pavement, but I did not.

WOMAN-CHILD

I was heavy, a sullen adolescent, charmless, menstruating, my waist-length hair parted in the middle, wearing a pair of chunky cord trousers, wide-legged with turn-ups, and a flamboyant satin blouse, hideous, giving me a blossoming bosomy look like Lana Turner.

That was August, three months before my fifteenth birthday, the summer holidays, a vacant stretch before the start of my fourth year at school. I was waiting for high summer weather, a last week or two of sunshine, but the rain kept on falling, warm rain out of a brown sky. I am trying to remember how I felt then. I felt bloated, my abdomen and breasts ripe like fruit, the waistband of the trousers cutting me. I am trying to remember how I spent those carefree weeks, but all I can recall is the rain falling and the feeling inside me, like a period pain.

On the first day of term the sun was shining. At lunchtime I smoked a joint in the cellar under the steps of the sixth-form house and wandered about the grounds in the sunshine. The first years, for whom term had begun the day before, were already familiar with the rituals of the place. They crowded round the mulberry tree, tasting the fat fruit ripening in its branches, their mouths and hands stained red, and played rounders on the little pitch beside the main road, hanging their jerseys on the fence behind which passers-by shuffled and took their places in the bus queue or turned to look at the schoolgirls in their short skirts and green knickers. A game of netball was in progress on the small tarmac court, and on the patch of grass by the back gates a group of girls sat cross-legged in a circle, trying to hypnotise each other, or meditate. In the shade of the school wall a girl was lying on a bench with her head in another's lap. I bought a cup of hot chocolate from the vending machine and sat on the grass, sipping the mauve froth floating on my drink and enjoying the sun on my head. I had spent the morning trying to understand the new timetable. I tried to copy the relevant parts onto the printed sheet we had been given but found it difficult; out of the forty periods of the week seventeen of mine were double-booked. I counted up the subjects I assumed I must be taking since I was unaware of having given any of them up and discovered they added up to thirteen. Bewildered by the impossibility of following the timetable in its entirety and unable to find my form mistress because she had taken the term off to have a baby, I decided to try and attend as many classes as possible for the next term. The good thing about this plan was the diversity. It was no longer a question of waking up in the morning and groaning at the boring inevitability of the day, the same old subjects in the same old order, knowing exactly week in week out what followed what, the terrible routine of school life. With this new plan of mine I could choose on a daily basis what I felt like doing. The idea was cheering. If I felt unable to face the rigours of Latin first thing on a Monday morning, there was now an alternative – double domestic science. The memory of kromeskis, a dish of minced meat balls wrapped in parcels of streaky bacon, coated with batter, and deep fried, or beef cobbler, a stew of braising steak topped with dumplings made out of a buttery scone mixture, browned in the oven, and the delicious bakewell tarts of last term, the creation of which I excelled at, made me feel hungry. I sipped the hot chocolate and smiled to myself, my eyes closed. When the bell began to ring I looked at my new timetable and saw the choice for that afternoon – maths followed by geography, French and Russian or maths followed by double physics followed by scripture, or any combination of those lessons, except it wouldn't be a good plan to wander into a class or walk out halfway through a double period. I decided to give up on the idea and bunk off, because autumn would soon begin and it seemed a waste to waste this lovely day.

I caught a train home from Camden Road station and looked out of the window at the backs of houses below me, the net curtains blowing out of open windows, clean washing billowing in weedy gardens, geraniums on windowsills, small squares of sooty lawn, walls of black brick, the canal, scrubby embankments, allotments and construction sites, the rows of orange-painted plant, serried diggers and cranes parked on gravel in bombed lots, the fronts of crumbling terraces, green awnings of shops, and blocks of postwar flats. I got off the train at Caledonian Road and Barnsbury station, walked down the leafy passage between the station and the main road, strolled along the Caledonian Road, turned left into Lofting Road, trailing my hand in the privet hedges growing over the low walls of front gardens, the weight of my schoolbag dragging on my shoulder, and turned left into Barnsbury Terrace, the street where we lived. There outside the house in an off-white car a man was sitting, staring out of the window at our front door. His hair was golden, honey-coloured, dry like straw, and the back of his neck was red. He was wearing a leather coat, in spite of the warm weather, brown, a stiff new shiny leather coat with Nazi epaulettes. I saw his profile, like a Greek god, that determined jaw and strong nose, those busy blond eyebrows, lips full and reddened, and his cheekbones hewn as out of stone. He must have seen me in the rear-view mirror, because he turned round. I saw his eyes then, light-blue eyes weak like water and knew it was the man. It was Klaus come back. I began to run, before he could get out of his car. I saw his moist blue eyes looking at me, at my flesh, soft under the long loose dress I was wearing, at my tits moving under the slippery material. The car door opened as I ran past, and his hand emerged, reaching out – I heard him whisper my name and felt his fingers brush my thigh but before he could get me I jumped down the steps to the back door, slammed it, turned the key in the lock and slid the bolt. I could hear my mother hurrying across the kitchen, and her tremulous voice, anxious and thin.

'What the hell is going on?'

At first I couldn't bring myself to tell her about the man. I sat down at the kitchen table, panting with fright, and she stood beside me, a hand on my shoulder, waiting for me to speak.

'What is it? What's the matter?'

I had been unaware, until that moment in the street when I saw the back of his neck, how I had come to fear Klaus in his absence. I felt as if I were going to shit in my pants. I shrugged my mother's hand off my shoulder and rose.

'I've got to go to the loo,' I said. 'Hang on. Hang on a minute.'

'I'll put the kettle on,' she said.

When I came out of the bathroom and sat down again my mother put a mug of tea in front of me.

'I've put some sugar into it. For the shock. You're as white as a sheet. You look like you've seen a ghost.'

It occurred to me suddenly that for her the return of the man might be a joyful occasion. I knew that at first she had missed him, cried in bed and longed for him to reappear, but over the years I had assumed she was over him. I thought she had forgotten him, particularly when Sarah was born, perhaps even hated him for his disappearance, the five-year absence, a wordless vacancy, unforgivable in my eyes. But my mother was different from me. Maybe the sight of that hulking great German, eyes brimming over with sorrow, weak with guilt and longing, maybe those blue smiling eyes would fasten on my mother and draw out of her whatever was left in the way of love. I did not want her to love that man, because I hated him. I was afraid that Klaus would make her hate me.

'It's Klaus,' I said. 'Remember?' What did she remember? I remembered him banging his head on the wall of my bedroom, and his voice, the voice of a coward, calling my name.

'Klaus?'

'Klaus,' I repeated.

'Don't tease me,' said Mother.

I was not teasing her. I jerked my head in the direction of the street.

'He's out there. In a white car. Waiting,' I said.

'Are you sure?' My mother's eyes were shining.

'I'm utterly and completely certain.'

My mother did not ask me why I was so frightened. She forgot to ask me why the sight of that boyfriend of hers nearly made me shit myself. She went into the bathroom to fetch the hairbrush, and began to brush her hair.

'I can't believe it,' she said. 'After all these years!'

Her hands were shaking. I realised that she was afraid too.

When she had finished brushing her hair she looked down at the shapeless dark clothes she was wearing and shrugged. I was trying to work out what she was afraid of. Was she frightened he would no longer find her attractive? Maybe it was just nerves. My mother was shy, unaccustomed to male visitors, awkward even with my father, who put in an appearance now and again. Was she scared the man would rape me?

'What shall I do?' She was asking my advice. 'Shall I wait until he rings the doorbell? Should I go to him?'

'Wait,' I said. I wanted her to blow his brains out. 'Wait and see.'

'Why can't he come and knock on the door like any normal person? It makes everything so awkward. Typical!' My mother forced out a little laugh. She looked girlish suddenly, rosy-cheeked, her eyes almost glazed.

'I'll have to go and pick the kids up from school soon,' she said. 'We can't just pretend he's not out there, can we? He won't wait forever. He might change his mind and go away. Perhaps he's nervous. Are you sure he's out there? What did you say to him?'

'Nothing,' I said. I wanted him to go away and never come back. I wanted him to die.

I drank the sweet tea cooling before me in one draught and banged the mug down on the table. My mother jumped.

'What did you do that for?' she asked. 'My nerves are in shreds as it is.'

'Sorry,' I said.

'Never mind.'

She began to rummage in a drawer, clumsily, spilling some of the bits and pieces crammed into it onto the floor.

'What are you looking for?'

'Cigarettes.'

I had never seen Mother smoke during the day.

'I've got some,' I said, offering her the packet.

We both lit up. She held her cigarette elegantly, between the tips of her index and middle fingers, holding it away from herself between puffs as if to protect herself from its noxious fumes, and I imitated her, without thinking, automatically.

'Will you come with me?' she asked suddenly, stubbing the cigarette out in the sink and running the tap. 'I'm going out there. Moral support.'

'All right.'

I unbolted the side door and turned the key in the lock. My mother was beside me, pressing the palms of her hands together in front of her face as if in prayer. Her posture was a little crooked – in the face of Klaus's return she had adopted a listing stance, self-effacing – her head was tilted to one side, and the left foot was twisted almost imperceptibly so that her weight settled onto the outside edge of her sole. I followed her up the steps and watched her go to him; she moved slowly, taking three small steps from our house to his car, and bent to face him, through the car window, only the dusty glass between them. He wound down the window and kissed her, full on the lips, their tongues squirming together in her mouth. When she drew back and took a breath he wound up the car window, opened the door and got out. They embraced, and I sat on the wall outside our house and watched. His big red hands were touching her, kneading her buttocks, squeezing her breasts, sliding between her thighs. I watched him cup his hand over her cunt proprietorially. I watched him grab handfuls of her newly-brushed hair. She had her back to me. Over her shoulder I saw his face; his eyes were open and I looked away – he was looking at me.

I went back into the house, went up to my room, and shut the door. I lay on my back on my bed like a corpse, motionless, staring at the ceiling. After about fifteen minutes I heard my mother calling me, her cheerful voice swooping and dipping in the stairwell like birdsong. I answered, shouting over the bannisters, and made my way downstairs. I greeted the man politely in the kitchen and kept my distance, sitting opposite him at the table. He was still wearing his leather coat. There were two bottles of vodka on the table, Blue Label Smirnoff, and he was already halfway down one of them, drinking the spirit neat out of a pint glass. He offered me some but I refused. Mother went to collect the children from school and Klaus made small-talk with me. He told me anecdotes and sea stories. When Mother returned with Sarah and Conrad, Klaus kissed and hugged them both and sent them out into the garden to play. He finished the first bottle of vodka, began to get maudlin, and started on the second. Soon he was too drunk to speak. When the second bottle was three-quarters empty he fell off his chair and lay unconscious on the floor. He was too heavy to lift so Mother and I dragged him by the legs through the doorless arch between the kitchen and the room next door and slid him under the table-tennis table. The table-tennis table was a present from my father. Mother covered Klaus with a blanket and went back into the kitchen to make the supper.

After supper while Mother was putting the children to bed Sue came in and I told her about Klaus. She crawled under the table and lifted up the blanket to have a look at him.

'Blimey,' she said, peering under the blanket. 'The size of him! He's enormous.' Sue looked up at me, her eyes popping out of her head. 'What did you say his name was?'

'Klaus.'

'He's gorgeous,' said Sue. 'Totally.' She smoothed the leather of his coat with the palm of her hand, and licked her lips.

'I think Mum feels the same way about him,' I said.

'I'm not surprised. Who can blame her. Do you think he'd fuck me if I gave it to him on a plate?'

'Probably,' I said. 'More than likely.'

'What about you?'

'What about me?' I asked, feigning incomprehension.

'I bet you'd like to go a round or two in the ring with him, wouldn't you, eh, little miss innocent?'

'Not my type,' I said.

'You're joking,' said Sue.

'I'm not, actually.'

'Weird,' said Sue. 'Totally weird.'

'He's more or less my stepfather, Sue,' I said.

'So?'

'So. My Mum's boyfriend. I don't fancy him anyway. Luckily.'

'Oh, right, point taken,' said Sue.

'And you can leave him alone for a start,' I said.

'Brownies' honour,' said Sue, tucking him in under the chin with the blanket as if he were a child. 'He makes a pleasant change from your old man anyway, in the looks department. I've always adored blonds.' Sue was faking a French accent. 'No, seriously,' she added. 'It might cheer your Mum up to have a man around the house, a live-in lover, you know, a bit of company on a regular basis.'

'Maybe,' I said.

'Do I detect a note of dislike in your voice?'

'He fancies me,' I said.

'He's only been here for a couple of hours. What makes you think he'd fancy you anyway, fatso?'

'He does. You wait. It's a fact.'

'Oh dear. That's heavy.'

'I know,' I said. 'What a drag.'

That night I jammed a chair under the doorknob of my room in case the man recovered consciousness in the middle of the night and came upstairs to get me. I slept fitfully, troubled by nightmares. I dreamt I was nursing a baby in my arms, a miserable baby that would not stop crying. I looked down at the baby I was comforting and saw it was my mother I held in my arms, the head of my mother, wrapped in a shawl, her red eyes full of tears.

In the morning I woke up, dressed, and went downstairs to

have a wash and a cup of tea before I set off for school. The front door was open and Mother was standing on the doorstep, holding a bundle of jerseys and gym shoes against her chest.

'Conrad! Sarah! Get a move on. It's time to go!' she called.

'Hi, Mum,' I said, leaning to one side of the staircase to make way for the two youngest children, who were stampeding down the stairs.

'Hi,' she said, smiling at me. 'Klaus is in the kitchen. Make him a cup of tea, would you? I'll be back soon.'

The leather coat was hanging over the bannister, limp like a dead animal. Klaus was sitting at the kitchen table, smoking a cigarette and sipping a cloudy solution of soluble aspirin. As I walked across the kitchen towards the stove he spoke to me in a small taut voice.

'Give me a kiss.'

'No.'

He stood up slowly and moved towards me, one hand caressing his forehead as if to relieve pain.

'Darling,' he said, holding out his other hand.

'Forget it, Klaus,' I said.

'It's been a long time. A long long time,' he said, sighing and returning to his place. Then he groaned and took another sip from the chalky glass. 'Why so uptight? You missed me, baby?'

'No.'

'I missed you, baby. Baby, you will never know or understand how much.'

'Don't call me baby,' I said.

'Wow! Don't hurt me,' he said. 'You really cut me up. Don't be cruel.'

I made a derisive noise by blowing air out of my nose, narrowed my eyes and gave him a dirty look.

'I love you,' he said.

'I don't love you.' I could remember the longing for him I used to feel as a child, how I tried to please him, the pleasure he gave me when he held me in his arms.

'You are a woman now,' he said. 'Beautiful. Kiss me.'

'No.'

'So shy. My shy baby. My little virgin woman.' Again he rose from his chair and came towards me. I backed up against the sideboard, leaning away from him to avoid the fumes of his breath, the big blond head moving closer, his lips.

'One kiss? Please. Pretty please. Very pretty please.'

I leant forward and touched his cheek with my lips.

His skin was weatherbeaten, a little leathery, the bristles pale and sharp like hogshair. His breath smelt of vomit.

'Thank you,' he said, his eyes full of tears.

I offered him a cup of tea and went into the bathroom. While I was brushing my teeth I could hear him singing a melancholy German folksong, the high notes quivering with sentiment, a song I had not heard since I was a child. Then he began to ask me questions. I could only just hear what he was saying because I had shut the bathroom door. I pretended not to be able to hear him at all.

'Hey, baby, you still a virgin? Have you got yourself a boyfriend yet? Are you on the pill? Do the boys love you? I bet you get hot for it.'

I didn't answer. When I emerged from the bathroom I picked up my schoolbag and hurried across the room towards the door. Klaus came after me, breathing heavily, and grabbed me from behind, sinking the ends of his fingers into the flesh of my sides, pressing himself against me.

'Come on, sexpot. You are hot. Answer me. You can tell me. Don't be shy. Do you like it? Who's been inside you? Don't the boys find this little belly a turn-off? How many have you had? Come on. Tell me. You clean, my little baby? You choosy? I bet they prefer the slender little girlies. Not me, baby. I can take it. Hit me. Come on, baby, you can tell me. Trust me. Describe it to me. Where you been, huh? What they do to you? Tell me. Turn me on. Turn me on.'

I lifted my knee and kicked out behind me, grazing his shin with my heel.

'Fuck off, Klaus,' I said, wriggling out of his loosened grasp. I ran out of the door and into the street. I kept on running in case he was following me until I was out of breath.

That night Sue and I went to see a band playing in the downstairs bar of the Hope and Anchor. When we arrived the Betty Wright tune 'Clean Up Woman' was playing on the jukebox; it was one of my favourite records at the time, and Sue and I had worked out a little dance routine to it – we stood back to back and bumped, turned face to face and clicked our fingers, and so on, standing in front of the stage and getting in the mood, drinking Pils out of the bottle and laughing hilariously. The cellar was smoky, full of long-haired pub-rock freaks, moody Islington weirdos, and trendies in their glad rags. The band was called Kokomo, a funky vocal harmony group I had heard several times before. When they bounced out of the dressing room onto the stage wearing berets and earrings we raised our hands above our heads and screamed. The first number began and we danced, holding hands and doing a sort of stumbling jive. In unison we spun round, treading on the toes of the audience, giggling, being uncool. With my arms raised above my head and a big smile on my face I stamped and hopped from leg to leg, spun again and caught Sue's hands as she flung past me. At the end of the song the saxophone wailed and tailed off in a series of staccato barking notes and I spun again, the faces of the audience blurring round my head. A pair of eyes in the crowd reminded me of Klaus. I blinked and spun once more and there he was, leaning against the wall by the gents, a glass in his hand. I felt afraid, angry, and ridiculous, like a child caught showing off. He was watching me, wearing a white suit, his hands in his pockets. The band tuned up and played another song, and another, and I went on dancing. I could not stop; I strutted and spun provocatively, his eyes on me. I wanted to stop dancing, to hide from him, to die – I did not want him to see my breasts wobbling, my bum wiggling, the sweat making my dress stick to me. Sue saw him too. She turned to face him, tossing her head back so that her hair floated, shaking her chest at him, and pouting for his benefit, a sad sort of defiant pout, teasing him – a piss-take. When he walked past us on the way to the gents I saw that he had an erection in his trousers. I knew he was going into the gents for a wank.

So he took to following me, standing behind me at parties, unsmiling, uninvited, drinking vodka, leaning against dark walls, behind pillars, watching me. I tried to behave as if he wasn't there, to carry on as normal, ignoring those horrible watery eyes fixed on me; I refused to catch his eye or to acknowledge his presence, nor did he try to speak to me. He never appeared in the Nazi coat, perhaps realising that such a high-profile garment would make it hard for him to slip unnoticed into my social life. He bought himself some new clothes, a pair of tight jeans, an Indian shirt, and a floppy jacket made out of faded pinkish material, in an attempt to blend into his new surroundings, or to make himself more attractive. I was always uneasy. I pretended I didn't know him, and he made a habit of leaving before I did, leaving suddenly so that when I turned round he was gone. I learnt to be cautious, and gave up walking around at night on my own. I was always looking over my shoulder, in the familiar streets where I had grown up, peering around me into the darkness, looking for him. And when I got home, there he was, sitting in the kitchen with my mother drinking vodka, or lying beside her in her bed.

This continued for several weeks and then stopped, quite suddenly. I thought he had given up, lost interest, or gone off me.

At the beginning of November it was Klaus's birthday. To celebrate he decided to take us on a family outing to a Greek restaurant in the Essex Road. I wore his white suit. It was too big for me round the middle and a little tight on the thigh but I hitched up the trousers with a belt and kept the jacket buttoned up throughout the meal. I can't remember why I was wearing that suit. I felt very uncomfortable inside it; people were looking at me in the restaurant; I did not like the feeling of the stiff seam between my legs; and my mother was obviously upset. I wanted her to put her foot down before we drove off in Klaus's white car, to shout at me, to tell me to go up to my room and take it off, to scold Klaus for encouraging me to be so stupid, for hurting her feelings and coming between us, but Mother said nothing. She gave me little sarcastic smiles, and watched as Klaus made an attempt to eat daintily. His big hands dwarfed the stainless-steel cutlery, and he was holding his knife in the way I knew my mother loathed. She was leaning away from him, perhaps because she found the noise of his chewing disgusting. Loudly he dropped his knife and fork onto the table and ripped apart his large kleftiko with his teeth. Louis had taken two tabs of acid before the meal began but still managed to eat a mixed kebab, salad, and rice. The rest of us had shish kebab, delicious meat charcoal-grilled with herbs, but I couldn't finish mine – I had no appetite.

It was Sunday afternoon. I had just woken up, emerging from a drug-induced sleep, dreamless, lying curled up in my bed, unwilling to move in case I dislodged the remains of the blurring anaesthetic dullness hanging on in my head. I closed my eyes, shutting out the dreary day already darkening outside my window, and took small shallow breaths, each exhalation a little silent sigh. I could hear footsteps on the stairs, children's footsteps, so I pulled the covers over my head. The door of my room opened, and Flora was shouting at me.

'Are you still alive? Mum said to check if you were still alive.'

She walked across my room and kicked the leg of my bed.

'Wakey wakey time slob.'

I groaned to let her know I was not dead and waited until she had gone away. The dull pall in my head began to disperse. My head hurt. I coughed up some lung gunk and spat it into a paper handkerchief. I needed a bath. Rising slowly, my eyes half-closed, I managed to get to my feet and lean against the wall beside my bed. I picked up a big towel that lay on the floor at my feet, wrapped myself in it, and staggered down the stairs. I nodded and smiled as I passed my mother and the man on my way to the bathroom – they were sitting at the kitchen table reading the papers and drinking tea. I looked at myself in the mirror while the bath was running. My cheeks were smooth and flushed pink, flawless, because I had slept so deeply. When the bath was full I lowered myself into the water, taking pleasure from my weightlessness. I stayed in the water until it began to cool, let a little out, then topped up the bath with more from the hot tap. The heat was so soothing. My feet were red like boiled lobsters. I was enjoying the lapping of the steaming water. Someone was knocking on the door.

'Get a move on,' said my mother. 'You are not the only person in this family. Hurry up in there.' Again she rapped on the door with her knuckles.

'Keep your hair on,' I said, heaving myself out of the bath. I felt a bit dizzy, and I was pink all over, pink and shiny like a baby. I wrapped myself in the towel, opened the door, and walked through the kitchen to the stairs.

'Any tea in the pot?' I said, hesitating.

'Yes,' said Mother.

I got myself a mug, filled it up, and sat down at the table. Mother and Klaus were ignoring me, hiding behind their papers. When I had finished my tea, I put the mug in the sink and went upstairs to my room. I put on my purple Biba bra and a pair of green knickers, the only ones that were clean, and began to look through the clothes hanging on the back of my door for something to wear. My mother was mounting the stairs, the rhythm of her weary footsteps easily recognisable. She opened the door of my room, startling me, and stood and stared at me in my bra and pants.

'What exactly is your game?' she said.

'What?' I said stupidly.

'What are you playing at?'

'What do you mean?' My head was aching now, and I covered myself with a blanket.

'Don't come running to me if you get what you're asking for.'

'What do you mean?'

'Deliberately provoking him. Walking round in a towel. You know exactly what I mean. You're not a child. No wonder he's like he is. Don't act innocent. You're not fooling anybody.'

I sat down on the bed and chewed the corner of the blanket. I felt like a child. I tried to examine my conscience but my head was woolly, my thoughts humming and inaccessible inside my overheated head like mental hieroglyphics, an uncracked code. I tried to look into my thoughts to find the answer to the question she was asking me, the question I was asking myself, but I couldn't remember what I was defending myself against. I couldn't remember the question.

'You silly little fool,' she said. 'How could you?'

'I didn't,' I said. 'I didn't mean it. I forgot.'

'What do you mean you forgot? Forgot what? That you're a woman, that he's a man? Go on, explain, tell me. Tell me.'

I was unable to explain myself. She did not understand. She

knew he was after me and yet she let him live in our house. He was after me and she said it was my fault. His unwanted attentions were not as hurtful as her lack of understanding. I began to cry.

'Go on, cry. And well you might, young lady,' she said.

That evening I was lying on the mattress where she slept in the sitting room, watching the telly, when Klaus came in and lay down beside me. He put his arm round me, the upper part of his body lying over me, and began to breathe loudly in my ear, leaning against me, squashing me beneath the weight of his shoulder and side. I told him to get off, to fuck off and leave me alone. He said nothing.

'I'll give you ten to get off me,' I said, and began the countdown. I stopped at six and warned him.

'If you don't get off me by the time I reach nought I'll scream.'

He was unable to leave me alone. He couldn't move.

'Five. Four. Three. Two. One.'

At first my throat contracted, dreamlike, and nothing came out of my open mouth. In the moment of silence it was as if Klaus were forgiven. Then I began to scream, louder than I have ever screamed before or since, and the wild wordless call gave me pleasure. My pleasure confused me. I punched and struggled, the man's breath moistening my neck, but he didn't get off until my mother appeared in the doorway, a hand raised to her grey face in an anxious gesture, as if she were stroking herself. Klaus pushed past her into the hall, and she ran after him. I sat on the edge of the bed, uncertain whether she would offer me comfort, apologise, or blame me when she returned. I heard them talking together in the hall, hissing at each other, but I could not understand what they were saying. Then the front door slammed; it made the house shake. My mother came into the room and sat down beside me on the bed.

'Happy now?' she said. 'Satisfied?'

'Has he gone?' I asked.

'Yes.'

'If he comes back I'm going to leave home,' I said.

'He said he's going to go and jump off Tower Bridge.'

'Are you being serious?'

'He did it before once, when you were little, before we went abroad. They fished him out, the River Police, in a sort of net they have for saving people.'

'Why don't you save him, run after him or something?' I asked.

'I don't know. He's gone in his car.'

'You could get a taxi.'

'I suppose so.'

Mother was crying. The end of her nose was red and shiny.

'You don't care, do you?' she said.

'No, I don't. I hope he dies. He hasn't got the nerve anyway.'

'It's your fault,' she said. 'You are cruel and heartless.'

Shortly after Klaus went away I found a piece of paper tucked behind my mother's bed, a page from a letter in her handwriting or perhaps the result of a sleepless night, one of those nights spent sitting up in bed with the light on, crying and writing down painful feelings in an attempt to make sense of things.

I want to run away with Klaus. I want to leave the kids behind. They can fend for themselves. I can no longer endure this misery. I feel so unloved, so guilty, so unlovable, so lonely. I know he loves me, he tries, but I feel like shit. I feel like a piece of shit. If we were on our own together, I know we could be happy together.

I never saw Klaus again. I imagined his head bobbing on the water, that golden head like the blond in *The Man from Uncle*, his square jaw and Aryan cheekbones floating in the insidious drag of the oily Thames, his watery eyes looking sadly across the surface at the peeling dredgers, navigational tugs and pleasure boats passing by. I imagined the cold, the smell of silted mud and oil and filth, the toxic froth, dead fish, the lethal undertow dragging him into the depths, his whole life passing by in front of his eyes like a film, his lungs filling with water, soaking up the poisonous water like a sponge – I imagined his death, the dead body rising to the surface, a flaking and bloated corpse, discoloured, decomposing, the blue eyes open, staring blindly at the sky. I imagined his tabloid drowning, the headlines of the *Sun* and the *Mirror*, the two-inch headlines, or a few column inches, then nothing. In fact he was fished out by the River Police, a replay of his first suicide attempt, but I never saw him again.

Sue moved back home just before Christmas because her father was hospitalised; he broke a leg in the course of duty, put his back out, and contracted pneumonia; her mother was lonely, making her way back from the hospital in the dark, and wanted someone to come home to, some company to see her through the long evenings. The following summer Dawn married Ernest and gave birth to twins. Sophie left Louis, unprepared to endure his unreasonable behaviour any longer, and went to live in Wales. About that time I fell in love myself, and left home.

Now I am thirty. Here are my stars for today in the *Evening Standard*.

The person you are today bears no resemblance to the individual you were a few weeks ago, and if you look for and anticipate the

best, then current upheaval is guaranteed to provide you with
the security you desire.

I had a dream last night that I was reborn. Two rooms, people
milling about. I returned from upstairs and found that the food
I had cooked had been served up in my absence before it was
ready. More people were arriving. Some brought with them
their own food, pre-prepared, on cling-film covered plates. I
was angry with my mother because it was her fault. I was cold.
I was trying to choose a jersey from a pile on a chair, getting
angrier, more and more childish, because I was unable to find
one that looked comfortable. I was getting younger and
younger, more and more furious, and then my mother had to
suffer terrible pain on my behalf. I inflicted it on her.
Afterwards I knew I had been reborn. I saw it written on a
piece of paper, in my handwriting. A man was involved,
lessening the pain, holding my/her soft sides. He was a kind
man, loving and gentle. The words on the piece of paper were
true, powerful, luminous with significance. In the dream I felt
free. When I woke up the feeling stayed with me.

Then I went back to sleep and dreamt I was married. My
husband was in bed beside me, breathing quietly – I had just
conceived; the child inside me was moving about a little bit,
kicking me. My husband began to read to me, his voice like
music. I woke up, it was three o'clock in the morning, I was
wide awake, so I got up and made myself a cup of tea, because I
did not want to go back to sleep and lose the blissful feeling of
the dream.

Sometimes I catch a glimpse of a Klaus lookalike, a tall man
with a pair of broad shoulders in a brown leather coat
disappearing into a lift just as the doors shut, a head of honey-
coloured hair moving towards me through a crowd, or two sad

eyes, like his, watery blue, watching me out of a white car as I hurry to cross the road, but these Klaus-like visions mean nothing to me now; I am no longer afraid.

I rang Sue the other day out of curiosity, to find out how things had turned out for her. I hadn't spoken to her for fifteen years.

'I'm still in the betting shop,' she said.

'What about Steve?' I asked. 'Did you wait?'

'I waited for him for seven years,' she said. 'It wasn't too bad. Every summer we met up for a fortnight and went on holiday together, somewhere nice. He paid. Spain, Italy, Portugal, you know, somewhere hot. Then four months before the end of his contract, we were due to get married that Christmas, I got a card from him. He had met a girl in a bar in Marseilles. She was French, a girl of seventeen, he was madly in love, they were getting married. "By the time you get this I will be a married man," he said. "I will always love you. Maybe we will meet again one day, you never know. Keep your pecker up. All the best. Steven." I read the card over and over again. I learnt it off by heart, trying to make it sink in. It took me a long time to get over it,' she said.

We chatted for a while. She was still living at home with her mother, her father was dead, and after I put the phone down I shed a few tears.

Today I received a postcard from my mother. She is on holiday in Ireland, visiting her uncle Ron. The postcard shows an Irish woman, large, proud, almost smiling, a tasselled plaid scarf crossed on her chest. The photograph is titled 'Lady with Irish Cloak'. On the other side is my mother's message.

Dearest Rose, it's rather nice here – yesterday I went to a horse show, there were the most gorgeous horses you have ever seen, just being led around by ordinary people, Connemara ponies and Irish drafthorses. Its very quiet here but beautiful as ever. The Lady with Irish Cloak reminds me of you. Much love Mum.

Last Christmas Eve, shortly before midnight, while returning from a Christmas party, I saw a man on his knees in the street, supported on either side by two stooping friends who were trying to raise him up off the pavement, helping him get to his feet. The sight reminded me of a photograph I cut out of a newspaper years ago, when I was at sixth-form college, a picture of a boxer called Dave 'Boy' Green, collapsed after a fight, his manager holding him up on one side, his trainer on the other, a ringside pietà as moving to me as any picture of Jesus after crucifixion. Anyway when I looked more closely at the man on his knees in the street I saw it was an old flame of mine, born on Christmas Day 1957, out celebrating the advent of Christmas, his birthday. Once he was standing up we hugged each other under the yellow light of a streetlamp and went our separate ways. I used to love to hear him sing, because he has a beautiful voice, and because I myself can't sing anything except the hymns and folksongs I learnt when I was a child.

I knock at the half-closed door and push it open. Olive is sitting in an armchair, surrounded by flowers, wearing a grass-green shiny tracksuit, her newborn baby at her breast. The baby is a girl. Olive's nipple is dark brown, beautiful as a flower. She pushes it into her baby's mouth, and her eyes are brown too, clear eyes, calm, full of love and happiness. She looks down at her feeding baby, looks up at me, and smiles.

'How you doing, woman-child?'